The Billionaire's Salvation

THE BILLIONAIRE'S OBSESSION
Max

J. S. SCOTT

The Billionaire's Salvation
The Billionaire's Obsession ~ Max
By J.S. Scott

Copyright © by J. S. Scott, 2013

ISBN: 978-1-939962-34-8 (ebook)
ISBN: 978-1-939962-38-6 (Trade Paperback)

Edited by Faith Williams—The Atwater Group
Cover Design by Cali MacKay – Covers by Cali

This one is for all of my incredible friends who have supported my writing and who bring me so much joy every single day: Melissa, Clara, Judy, Chrissy and Rita. I'm grateful to have such strong, supportive and awesome women as friends. You girls rock!

-Jan

Contents

Prologue

February, 2011

Max Hamilton stood on the sandy stretch of beach at the back of his home, shivering as he stared blankly at the ocean, and scowling at the water crashing to the shore as though it were the enemy. The night was nearly pitch-black, but there was enough illumination from the moon and stars to see the churning ocean in front of him. In a very elemental way, it *was* his nemesis, the body of water that had taken Mia away from him. And at the moment, he resented every drop of water in the Atlantic Ocean. Somewhere, his wife was lifelessly floating in this body of water, buried in a watery grave, and he could feel her moving farther and farther away from him. It was as though she had torn his heart from his chest and carried it with her, and he was standing here helplessly, bleeding out from the gaping wound.

He put a hand to his chest and rubbed, but it didn't stop the excruciating pain.

No...dammit. She can't be gone. I thought I had plenty of time to figure out my irrational emotions. I thought I could work everything out of my system and love her the way she deserved to be loved.

His legs weak, he dropped to the sand on his ass, the moisture sinking into the denim of his jeans, but he ignored it, his gaze fixated on the water. He was too numb to feel the external elements, too devastated to care, his whole being focused on Mia, as though he could bring her back by sheer force of will. He ignored not only the chill of the wind buffeting his body, which was clad only in a t-shirt and jeans, but the mosquitoes making a meal of his exposed flesh, and the excruciating sense of loss that was so painful he had to block it or go insane.

Every muscle in his body was tense, his fists clenched, his brain trying to keep his emotions in check. To mourn would mean that he was accepting the fact that Mia was gone forever, and he didn't want to believe it. Screw it. He'd stay in denial. If he accepted that she had drowned off the shore of this very beach, he'd never live through the agony of it.

Max Hamilton didn't cry. Never had. Even when his parents had been killed in a tragic accident, he'd buried the urge, knowing they'd be ashamed of him. No Hamilton wallowed in emotion or let it overrule logic and control. He knew his parents had loved him, but they had been born into wealth, and they'd always taught him how to behave with decorum and moderation. His mom and dad always said he was a perfect child, and they were proud of him. Having been adopted, Max had always wanted to stay perfect, and he'd tried, even after they'd died. The habit of trying to stay aloof and detached was something he associated with love and approval. Now, he wasn't so sure, his gut telling him that Mia may have died never knowing exactly how he felt about her.

Unfortunately, he wasn't feeling very level or solid at the moment, and his usual Hamilton demeanor was deserting him completely.

Mia had disappeared from this spot exactly one week ago—her bag, clothing, and phone left on this stretch of sand. She'd always loved to take a quick swim here, calling it her own little piece of paradise.

Closing his eyes, Max pictured her face, her mischievous expression and teasing smile. Christ, how he hated it when she went swimming alone, did things that he considered dangerous. He'd lectured her like a teacher might do with a student, but she'd always laughed at him, cajoling him out of his anger, telling him he was too serious and worried too much. Problem was, he never could stay angry with her. Damn woman had had him wrapped around her little finger almost from the moment they had met, and he had happily let her do it. He'd cautioned her when she'd done things that worried the shit out of him. And then, he'd let her go on her merry way, let her think he was only mildly concerned, when in reality, he was fucking terrified of losing her.

He was the serious one, the man who did everything cautiously and logically. And Mia…ah Mia: she made him happy, she made him laugh, she made him whole, and she made him want to lose control completely. But he never had. Not once. He'd managed to leash the bestial instincts she brought out in him. Just barely.

"It was our deal," he whispered hoarsely, although the actual agreement had never been official or talked about. "I handled the serious stuff and you helped me lighten up." She made him laugh when he got too stuffy, and he grounded her. Together, they were perfection. Or maybe Mia was perfection, and she just made him a happier man. It didn't matter that he had to fight the urge to turn into a caveman and conquer her constantly, wanting to drag her back to his lair. But she had never known about that, the secret part of him that really wanted to be free.

Because I didn't want to scare her away.

He laid back and covered his face with one arm, releasing a strangled, tortured groan. Emotions warred inside him, each fighting for dominance in a mind filled with chaotic thoughts: anger, despair, denial, and pain. Unfortunately, the agony filling his heart and soul were winning, held back somewhat by denial.

She's not dead. She's not dead. I needed more time.

Squeezing his eyes tightly shut to decrease the burning sensation beneath his eyelids from tears he refused to shed, he swallowed a sob that was rising in his chest. He and Mia were a pair, and he didn't work without her. They'd been married for two years, clicking together like puzzle pieces that were only complete when they were interlinked, almost from the moment they'd met. He'd never believed in love at first sight or an instant connection...until he'd met his wife. They were complete opposites in so many ways, yet they belonged together. That feeling had been there for him from the very beginning of his relationship with his wife, but he'd stayed in denial, thinking that the way he'd felt about her would eventually subside to a manageable level.

It never did. And honestly, Max knew it never would have. He had just been too big of an idiot to admit it.

Sitting up, he wrapped his arms around his knees and rocked, fighting against every rational thought that entered his head about his wife's disappearance. If he started thinking logically, he'd have to admit she was probably dead. Mia wouldn't disappear and not contact him. She might be a little careless with her own safety at times, ditching his security whenever she could, but she was never thoughtless. There was no way she wouldn't contact him unless she physically couldn't.

"Where are you, Mia?" he whispered huskily, his voice desperate. "Don't do this to me. Please. I need you."

I should have told her I loved her more often, spent more time with her instead of jetting from place to place in search of world domination and trying to hide the primitive instincts she brought out in me. I shouldn't have run away. She might have been able to deal with that part of me, just like she dealt with everything else.

In reality, he hadn't given her the chance. He'd never let himself completely open up to her, had never told her exactly how he felt. Now, when it was too late, he regretted it.

Rocking harder, he opened his eyes, and the tears finally flowed. He swiped an arm across his eyes, cursing angrily as he roughly removed the droplets from his ravaged face, but they kept returning, and that only pissed him off more.

Stumbling to his feet, he moved to the edge of the water and waded in, so damn tempted to lose himself in the ocean if it was the only way he and Mia could be together again.

She's not dead. She's missing. I'm not giving up on her!

"Mia!" His hoarse shout was carried away across the water by the brutal wind, his body shivering as he called desperately, "Come back."

No one answered, and he fell to his knees in the frigid water, letting it lap over his chest. His tears mingled with the water, and his hopelessness and anguish burst from his throat in a painful sob. And then another. And another.

The waves pushed his body toward the shore, and he let the momentum carry him. When he reached the sand, he crawled on his hands and knees for a short distance before collapsing on the beach.

Stop fucking crying. She's not dead. She's out there somewhere. You need to find her.

Coughing hard, he tried to stem the harsh sounds erupting from his mouth, angry that he was already mourning a wife who hadn't yet been proved dead. So what if the police and everyone else thought she was deceased? He wasn't giving up. He'd never give up.

There was no activity on her bank accounts, no sign she was still alive. But he wasn't going to stop until he found her. Barely sleeping since she had disappeared, he'd spent the last week tearing through Tampa looking for her, hiring private resources when the police were basically shaking their heads in resignation.

"I won't give up on you, sweetheart. I promise," he muttered, his lips gritty from the sand that was beginning to coat the inside of his mouth as he inhaled. "I'll wait forever."

His vision blurring, he stared determinedly at the crashing waves, exhaustion overwhelming him. He could see lights in the distance, boats passing through his line of vision in the dark night. Blinking, he tried to stay conscious, but blackness covered him and he succumbed to it, knowing he wasn't leaving this beach tonight. Maybe he never would. Maybe he'd stay here until he died or Mia came back to him.

The wet, shivering, bedraggled figure lay unmoving until daylight, opening his eyes in the morning and hoping that everything that had happened in the last week had only been a dream.

It wasn't…and when Max looked in the mirror the next day… he had to admit to himself that sometimes there were no second chances. Every so often, something or someone extraordinary came along in life and there was only a small window of opportunity to snatch it and make it your own. Unfortunately, he'd been a coward, afraid of change, and his "someone extraordinary" had been taken away before he could entirely claim her.

For the first time in his life, Maxwell Hamilton was left with regrets. And it was excruciatingly painful. Later, he might examine his life and figure out whether or not he really needed to be a robot that functioned with meticulous control and logic, doing only what was acceptable in his mind. But that would come later, after the pain subsided. Unfortunately, that day never came.

Chapter 1

The Present

"I don't want a woman, Maddie. I'm already married." Max fingered his platinum wedding band, a ring that had rarely left his finger since the day he'd gotten married, and would remain on the same damn finger even after he was dead. Technically, he *was* still married. Mia's body had never been recovered, nor had she been declared legally dead.

He took a deep breath and slowly let it out, savoring the smell of barbeque and the outdoors. They were having an "end of summer" picnic, a rare time when friends and family were able to get together in one of the local parks and act like kids again, and forget that they were a bunch of the wealthiest people in the world with more responsibility hanging over their head than the average person. Today, they could just be ordinary, and Max didn't want to have this conversation with his newfound sister. He just wanted to savor the fact that he actually *had* family, a sibling he had never known existed until earlier this year. Just for a few hours, he wanted to enjoy the company of the people he cared about and try not to think about the woman he'd lost. Finding Maddie had been a miracle, a gift that he didn't want to squander.

Maddie chewed on her lower lip, looking at him with a concerned expression across a picnic table to which they had been banished by Maddie's husband, Sam Hudson. Sam was barbequing and wanted his pregnant wife away from the fire. Max smiled, wondering how his friend and brother-in-law was going to survive this pregnancy with Maddie. She was only a few months along and Sam already treated her like she was as fragile as blown glass. He could only imagine how insanely protective Sam would become as her pregnancy progressed. It wouldn't matter that Maddie was a physician and perfectly capable of knowing what she could and couldn't handle; Sam would hover. Honestly, Max couldn't blame him. He was feeling more than a little brotherly protectiveness himself. His sister was thirty-five, two years his senior, and she wanted this baby so desperately. He'd definitely breathe a sigh of relief when the baby was safely delivered. Any other result would break Maddie's heart, and his sister had already had enough adversity to fight through in her life.

"I just want you to be happy," she answered softly, tugging nervously on a strand of her curly red hair.

Oh hell, he hated that sad look on her face, but somehow he needed to make her understand that he wasn't interested in a female companion. Sometimes there was no ecstatic happiness like she had with Sam. It definitely wasn't in *his* future. He'd had the love of his life... and had managed to fuck things up completely. His sister had been trying to hook him up with various women all summer, and it needed to stop. "I feel the same way about Mia as you feel about Sam. I loved her. I still do. Her death didn't change that. There isn't anyone else for me, Maddie. She was my one and only." Max knew Maddie would understand. After all, she had waited over a decade for Sam. "I can't be with anyone else. Not now. Not ever."

"You feel that way now, Max, but someday—"

"I'll feel exactly the same way next year, ten years from now, and every day after that." He wasn't going to bullshit her. Not anymore. In the past, he'd changed the subject every time she mentioned that maybe he should find some female company, but he wasn't backing down. Maddie's quest for his happiness was endearing, but misguided, and it only reminded him of what he'd lost. "If something happened to Sam, when would you be ready to be with someone else?"

Her face fell and Max felt like a complete asshole. The last thing he wanted to do was hurt Maddie. He knew she meant well and wanted him to be as happy as she was now with Sam, but he couldn't take it anymore and he desperately needed her to back off. He'd spent the last two and a half years trying to just stay sane, the pain in his chest never going away, trying to function every day and push through the agony of living without Mia. It was better not to think about romantic relationships at all. There was no happily ever after for him. There was only survival. And he was much better off working, exhausting himself into sleep, and being grateful for the family and friends he had. He didn't want another woman. There was no substitute. He just wasn't built that way. Apparently, he and his sister shared that same trait: fall in love once and it lasts forever.

"Never," Maddie admitted sadly, her hazel eyes meeting his, finally comprehending what he was trying to convey. "I'd never be ready because Sam was the only man for me. I understand. And I'm sorry. I just feel so damn helpless. I want to help, but I don't know what to do."

Max got up and moved around the table, seating himself beside his pregnant sister and taking her gently into his arms. He closed his eyes, savoring the feminine embrace of his compassionate sibling as she wrapped her arms around his shoulders and squeezed. His voice was husky as he told her quietly, "You already help me. Just by being my sister. I don't need anything else." He was lying, and he knew it. But what he needed wasn't possible. Mia wasn't coming back, and he needed to accept it. He just...never really had.

"Hey. You two better break it up before Sam comes over here and breaks both your arms and kicks your ass." The casual, masculine voice sounded behind them; his brother-in-law, Kade, was moving toward them with Tucker, Max's sad-looking hound dog—or rather, Mia's dog. Tucker was a stray that Mia had adopted, and Max had never really figured out his actual breed. He looked like a pathetic cross between a bloodhound and basset hound, a canine that did very little except eat and give Max disapproving looks with eyes that peered through a wrinkled face. He wasn't sure how Kade had even managed to get Tucker to move. The lazy, spoiled dog generally just gave anybody who wanted to go walking his doggie look of disdain and went back to sleep. The canine could be a pain in his ass, but Max had never been able to get rid of Tucker, no matter how many accusing looks the dog gave him, as if Max had been responsible for Mia going away. She had adored Tucker, and the ugly hound dog had been completely enamored of its mistress. Man and dog had called a truce for just that reason, had learned to tolerate each other. Max knew Tucker still pined for Mia, as if still waiting for her to come home. In that respect, man and hound were similarly pathetic. In some strange, screwed-up way, it made Max feel better knowing that there was another soul still mourning Mia's loss, even if it was a sixty-five pound, incredibly ugly dog.

Kade limped toward them, Tucker lumbering behind him. The dog was panting, its pink tongue hanging from its mouth as it plopped at Max's feet and gave him an irritated stare.

"It's not my fault. You went with him," Max answered Tucker's silent castigation, glaring back at the hound. Like Tucker didn't know Kade? His brother-in-law, Mia's brother, pushed himself on his mangled leg as though he had something to prove. When he'd had the motorcycle accident that had ended his stellar professional football career, his doctors hadn't even thought he'd keep his leg. But he did, and Kade was still in better physical shape than any man Max knew.

Max released Maddie, who smiled at Kade as he plopped his ass onto the bench beside her, leaving her sandwiched between them. "Did you two have a good romp?" she asked, reaching down to pet Max's pathetic hound. Tucker was already snoring, but released a satisfied doggie whimper as Maddie stroked his head.

"Yeah. Tucker completely wiped me out and worked me out. The dog sets a brutal pace," Kade answered facetiously and smiled at Maddie as she leaned up again, looking like he could hike at least another several miles without breaking a sweat. Max was positive that Tucker had waddled along at a snail's pace, which had no doubt irritated the hell out of Kade.

God, he reminds me so much of Mia.

Kade and Mia had the same deep blue eyes, blinding smile, and blond hair. At the moment, Kade's hair was disheveled and longer than usual, touching the collar of his incredibly ugly, garish floral shirt. For some reason, Kade had always been a prime candidate for the *Worst-Dressed* list. It certainly wasn't because he had no money. His brother-in-law was beyond wealthy, his net worth probably greater than Max's. He'd taken over the Harrison Corporation along with his twin brother, Travis, when their parents had passed away over four years ago, and he'd been a star quarterback for a Florida pro team for years before his accident, commanding a huge salary and lucrative endorsements. Max was willing to bet that even though the shirt looked like it needed to be tossed in the nearest trash can, it had a designer label. Honestly, Max was pretty certain that Kade dressed the way he did just to annoy his twin brother. Travis was completely anal and meticulous—traits that Max also had—which should have made him closer to Travis than Kade. But after losing Mia, Max and Kade had gotten closer, spent more time together. Kade had been willing to talk about Mia; Travis remained stoic and secluded.

"Well, it was very sweet of you to take Tucker for some exercise," Maddie told Kade, leaning over to peck him on the cheek.

"Hey, knock that off. Sam puts up with Max getting a little affection, but if you aren't related, you better keep your distance." Simon Hudson, Sam's younger brother, approached the table with his very pregnant wife, Kara, his voice holding a serious note of warning.

"We are related by marriage...sort of," Kade replied, grinning as Simon helped Kara step over the bench on the opposite side of the table and sit. "She's the sister of my brother-in-law. That should count."

Simon was frowning, his concern for his ready-to-pop-any-moment pregnant wife evident by the stressed look on his face. Kara was glowing, her face rosy from her walk with her husband. Simon finally glared at Kade as he sat beside his wife and commented gruffly, "Doesn't count. If you aren't related by blood, forget it."

Kara smacked her husband in the arm. "Kade's like family. Leave him alone, caveman. We happen to like it that he treats Maddie and I like sisters. I've made Kade and Max my honorary brothers."

Max barked out a laugh. "So can we come on over there and give you a brotherly little hug, Kara?" he asked, watching Simon carefully. Honestly, he really shouldn't bait the poor guy. Simon was obsessively jealous and his wife *was* nine months pregnant, but Max just couldn't help himself. Shooting Kade a conspiratorial glance, both men began to rise.

Simon growled—actually snarled—as Kade and Max stood.

Kara beamed, delighted, looking pleased with the idea of giving both men a brotherly hug.

"Come one step closer and you'll both end up in the hospital," Simon warned dangerously.

Max smiled, while Kade laughed uproariously. Yeah, it was definitely not nice to tease Sam and Simon about their women, but since neither Kade nor Max actually *had* a woman, it was just so entertaining to watch Simon's reaction. Both of them sat back down, knowing better than to push the jesting any further. Max had no doubt that Simon would make good on his promise.

"Just wait," Simon warned. "Payback sucks."

Max's smile faded. While Kade had recently been dumped by his longtime girlfriend, his brother-in-law *would* probably find a good woman someday and get paid back for teasing Simon. But Max knew *he* never would. And he'd never treated Mia the same way Sam and Simon treated their wives. His parents had loved him, given him everything an adopted child could ever want, and in return, he'd always tried to make them proud by behaving with control. Not that he hadn't wanted to go completely cave dweller on Mia at times—actually pretty much all the time—but he hadn't allowed those emotions to claw to the surface. He'd ruthlessly crushed those feelings, burying them deep inside him, and he had loved

Mia with the same tepid, felicitous affection his dad had shown his mom. But, Holy Christ, it hadn't been easy. Max knew his possessive, animal instincts had been there with Mia, snarling to get out, but he'd always hid them, constantly struggling to keep them leashed. Now, he wished he would have set them loose and loved her wholeheartedly. He'd been afraid of scaring her off, freaking her out with his irrational behavior. But watching the other men with their women, he wasn't entirely certain that she wouldn't have wanted him that way. Kara and Maddie seemed happy, entirely certain that they were loved. Had Mia felt that way? Max wasn't sure she had.

Sam brought over a huge platter of freshly cooked burgers and hotdogs. Picnic tables were hastily pushed together to seat everyone, the wood nearly groaning with the weight of all the people and enough food to feed a small army. Kade slid in next to him on his left, and Maddie slipped into the seat to his right.

Max's eyes scanned the crowd sitting at the table and then around the perimeters of the park, wanting to laugh at the amount of undercover security that surrounded them. Already knowing Sam and Simon would have the park surrounded, he hadn't bothered to include his small security team in this event. Now, he was really happy that he hadn't. It would have definitely been overkill. The Hudson siblings practically had an entire SWAT team around the park to guard their wives. Not that Max really blamed them. Maybe if he had been firmer with Mia about her security, maybe if he hadn't let her convince him that she didn't need to be followed every minute of the day, maybe…

He was reaching for a hamburger bun when he saw *her*, his hand stopping abruptly before it reached the platter, his entire body frozen in place as he met the stare of a woman about fifteen feet from him, her body still and half hidden by a palm tree. His heart surged and then plummeted to his feet as his eyes locked with hers, eyes so very much like Mia's. He might have been able to blow off the fact that her eyes were the same azure blue as his deceased wife's, but he couldn't ignore the sense of recognition he felt and saw reflected back at him from her gaze. *Sweet Jesus.* "Mia," he whispered huskily, his hand lowering to the table as he openly gaped at her.

Hearing Max's quiet declaration, Kade looked at Max, following the direction of his stare, looking at the woman for a moment and then back at Max. "Don't do this to yourself, man. It isn't her," Kade told him harshly.

Yeah. Sure. For the first year after Mia's disappearance, Max had seen her everywhere he went, in every crowd. But this wasn't the same thing. "I feel her," Max answered, his eyes never leaving the woman, his body tensing as he rose to his feet.

Kade grasped his arm. Hard. "Her eyes are the same color, but that's all. It isn't her. Look at her, Max. She has short, dark hair. She's thin. Nothing is the same except her eyes. There are lots of women with blue eyes. Stop torturing yourself. Mia's gone and she's never coming back." Kade's voice was low, grating, his head turned so only Max could hear him.

Max ignored him, shrugging off his brother-in-law's hold as he stood, the sorrow that he felt coming from the woman beckoning him, calling to him. Stepping over the bench seat of the picnic table, he kept his focus on her. The sense of recognition he felt made every sound fade around him until all he could hear was the thundering sound of his heart pounding in his ears, and all he could feel was the eerie sensation of knowing the woman who was so close to him, yet too far away.

Déjà vu.

Those were exactly the same sensations he had experienced the moment he'd first looked at Mia and had fallen into her deep blue eyes.

As he took a step toward her, she bolted. Breaking his gaze, she pivoted and started sprinting away from him, her slim, bare limbs exposed in a pair of shorts and a t-shirt, moving gracefully in quick, fast strides.

Dammit. No. Don't run. Please don't run.

Desperation seized him as his body kicked into motion, his feet pounding the dirt as he ran after her, covering the distance between them quickly. "Wait. I just wanted to talk to you," he yelled, close enough to almost touch her.

Her head jerked around while she was in motion, startled by his voice so close to her, her expression panicked. Concentration lost, she stumbled, not seeing the elevated sidewalk in front of her. She went down hard, her head the first thing to hit the pavement. Because she had been looking back at him, she'd never had a chance to throw out her arms to break her fall.

"Fuck." Max's breath left his body as he leaped to avoid landing on top of her, cringing as he saw her head connect with the cement as she went down. He slowed and turned, dropping to the ground beside her, hating himself for chasing after her like a madman and causing the brutal fall. "Are you okay?" he asked hoarsely, turning her body over gently, cradling her head.

She was dazed, her expression befuddled as though she was trying to figure out what had happened. "You didn't shave today."

It should have been an odd thing for her to say, but it wasn't. He used to be meticulous about shaving, sometimes having to do it twice a day to keep the stubble from his face. He didn't worry much about it anymore, shaving only once in the morning and ignoring his five o'clock shadow.

The sultry, confused voice flowed over Max and then sucker-punched him in the gut so hard he couldn't breathe, couldn't think. "Mia?" He could barely get her name past his lips as he gathered her fragile form into his arms, his whole body quaking with shock.

The woman shook her head, a gesture that looked like she was trying to clear her brain. "No. I'm not the woman you want," she said as she continued to shake her head, her expression going blank as her eyes fluttered closed and her entire body went slack in his arms, her head flopping against his chest.

Bullshit. You're exactly the woman I want.

As Max clasped her tighter against his chest, he whispered fervently, "No. Wake up. Stay with me." The palm cradling her head was damp, and as he moved it slightly away, it was saturated with blood from a cut on her head.

Head wounds bleed a lot. It might not be as bad as it looks. Stay calm. Oh hell, who am I trying to fool? She's out cold.

Sam, Simon, and Kade arrived as Max stood, holding the woman's slight weight in his arms.

"Have you lost your damn mind? Why did you take off like that?" Kade stared at the woman Max was holding. "What happened to her?"

"Fell. She's unconscious, smashed her head against the concrete. We need to get her to a hospital. Call an ambulance."

For once, Kade didn't argue, his hand diving into the pocket of his jeans for his phone.

Max started walking, his rational mind working automatically, knowing he needed to get her through the park and to the road where they could meet the ambulance. He could feel her warm breath against his skin, her pulse beating rapidly underneath his fingertips that were resting against her neck.

She's alive. Mia's alive.

That particular fact was astounding on more than one level, but Max knew he couldn't think about that now. He'd figure everything out eventually. Right now, Mia needed him to take care of her medical needs. If he didn't focus on that and only that...he'd totally lose it, and his famous Hamilton control would desert him completely.

Max moved as quickly as he could through the park, trying not to jostle the woman in his arms too much, Simon and Sam flanking him silently on each side. Kade was behind him, still on the phone, briskly directing emergency personnel to their location.

"I can carry her for a while," Sam said quietly, putting his hand on Max's shoulder to try to make him stop walking.

"No," Max growled. It would be a cold day in hell before he relinquished his hold on her. He'd just gotten her back. He wasn't letting her go. Shrugging off Sam's hand, he kept moving.

"You can't hang on to her until the ambulance gets here. It could take awhile." Simon tried to reason with him.

"The hell I can't," Max answered harshly, his hold tightening on his woman involuntarily as he lengthened his stride. "She's my wife.

I'll carry her as long as I need to." He needed to keep her, needed to hold her.

He didn't notice Sam and Simon's astonished looks as they both gaped at him like he'd suddenly lost his mind.

"You think that's Mia?" Sam asked, confused.

"It is Mia," Max answered confidently.

"Max, she doesn't look like Mia—"

Arriving at the parking lot, Max jerked his head around to look at Sam, telling him belligerently, "It's her." He knew his own wife. She smelled like Mia; she felt like Mia; she *was* Mia.

The woman in his arms began to stir just as Kade joined the three men. Sirens were wailing distantly, rapidly moving closer. "Ambulance is coming," Kade muttered, shoving his hands in his pockets, his expression concerned as he looked at Max. "Max, I know you think that's Mia, but you must know that she really isn't."

Max watched Mia's eyes flutter open slowly, blinking like she was trying to focus her vision and looking around warily. "What happened? Why are you carrying me?" she rasped.

"You fell and hit your head, sweetheart," Max answered softly.

"Can you put me down please?" she requested, squirming.

Scowling, he answered, "Not happening. You're hurt."

Irritated, she looked at her brother. "Kade, can you tell Max that I'm fine? Where did you get that horrible shirt? I think that's worse than the one with the purple birds." Her confused eyes moved over Simon and Sam. "Why are Simon and Sam here? Where the hell are we? Dammit! I feel like I got run over by a semi-truck." She rested her head against Max's shoulder and closed her eyes, no longer arguing about Max holding her, her lucid moment apparently over.

The four men all looked at one another, none of them moving as they stared at the female Max was holding.

"Holy shit," Simon and Sam grumbled in unison.

Max's heart accelerated, his mouth going dry. He found himself incapable of speech as he tried to wrap his mind around what was happening...and failed miserably.

Kade yanked the phone from his pocket and punched one of the buttons. Raising his voice to be heard over the sirens of the arriving ambulance, he shouted into the phone, "Travis? I need you to meet us at the hospital. We think we found Mia, and she's alive."

Maddie, Kara, and the rest of the guests for the picnic arrived, everyone talking at once as a paramedic hopped out of the ambulance and rushed over with the gurney. Max reluctantly laid Mia on the board that rested on top of the pristine sheet, but he gripped her hand and never let go. Ignoring the chaos around him, he followed wherever his wife was going. Hopping into the ambulance, he sat near her head and let the paramedic do his job, but he gripped her hand, squeezing it lightly, needing to keep the connection.

"Are you hurt, sir?" the brisk voice of the young medic asked.

The question barely penetrated the fog around Max's brain. Slowly, he glanced down at his t-shirt, realizing he was covered in blood from Mia's head wound.

"No," he said huskily, shaking his head. "Not anymore."

The perplexed young man in uniform looked at Max for a moment and shrugged, obviously convinced that the blood on Max belonged to Mia. Setting back to work, he stemmed the blood from Mia's head wound, stabilized her head and neck, and started peppering Max with medical questions about his wife.

Yanking himself brutally from his own thoughts, Max went into autopilot, answering every question, responding coherently, giving the paramedic every bit of information he could to help Mia.

Mustering every bit of the Hamilton control he could find, Max calmed and buried his emotions. It should have been easy. It was something he'd done most of his life. But right now, it was an enormous effort, one that he almost didn't care whether he accomplished or not.

Do it for Mia. She needs you to be sensible and get a grip on yourself.

With that thought, Max was able to totally rein himself in, become the rational man she had always expected.

By the time the ambulance arrived at the hospital, Max was in command of himself; the only signal that he hadn't quite managed to completely bury his emotions was the steadfast, unwavering grip he retained on Mia's hand.

By some unknown phenomenon, Max knew he was actually getting a second chance. As improbable as it was, his wife had been given back to him, and he wasn't going to fuck it up this time.

His face grim, he never left Mia, even when he was instructed to wait somewhere else. He'd waited long enough. He had his wife in his grasp, and he wasn't ever letting her go again.

Chapter 2

"I've talked to all of her doctors, Max. Even the consulting psychiatrist. Her traumatic brain injury is fairly mild; she's experiencing some symptoms of post-concussion syndrome with retrograde amnesia. She really doesn't remember the last two and a half years or what occurred during that time." Maddie was using her doctor's voice, but her expression was concerned as she sat down next to Max in the hospital waiting room and covered his hand with hers.

Max released an exhausted breath before replying, "Could you put that in layman's terms, Maddie? What does it mean?" Running a frustrated hand from his forehead to his jaw, he looked at his sister, unable to hide his pleading expression. He wanted someone to tell him that Mia was going to be okay. Anything else was just not acceptable.

"It means when she smashed her head into the cement, it scrambled her brain around inside of her skull and screwed up some of the tiny cells that exist inside the brain. She's fine, Max. Really. There's nothing significant on her MRI. The headache and dizziness will eventually subside and her memory should come back." She removed her hand from his as Sam entered the room with a cardboard holder filled with foam cups of coffee, silently handing both him and Maddie a cup before taking one for himself and plopping beside his wife.

Max knew he should feel some sort of relief from hearing the words Maddie was saying, but every time he saw the vulnerability on Mia's face, it made him want to kill someone. Problem was, he had no idea *who* to hurt for what had happened to his wife. Hell, he didn't even know *what* had happened to her. Most of the time, he didn't dare question the fact that she was back and whole. But he couldn't help having a few moments of doubt, wondering where in the hell she'd been, what she'd gone through during the last few years. He was a man of reason, and nothing was making sense.

As though reading his mind, Sam commented slowly but dangerously, "We'll figure out what happened, Max."

Max could hear in Sam's tone the words he didn't say aloud... *and the bastard or bastards responsible will pay if they hurt her.* Max looked across his sister and saw Sam's expression. As the two men's eyes connected, Sam nodded once at Max, letting him know he meant business. Max inclined his head slightly, acknowledging Sam's support, so damn glad that someone understood his irritation and frustration, his raw male need to get revenge for whatever had happened to Mia. Yeah, he wasn't sure she had even been hurt, but someone had taken her away, and he wanted that person's head right now.

"You need to sleep, Max. You've been here for two days straight. Go home and get some rest. Mia can go home in the morning." Maddie's voice was pleading, her eyes troubled.

Oh, hell no. They'd need an entire damn army to drag him away from Mia. She was confused and scared, and though Maddie didn't know it, that was a rarity for Mia. He needed to be here with her. His wife was back, and nothing was taking her away from him again. With the uncertainty of what exactly had occurred, why she had disappeared, there was no way he was leaving her. "I'm staying. I'll sleep when we go home," he answered stubbornly, pulling the lid from his coffee and taking a healthy gulp. "You two need to take off. I'll be fine here." Shit, he wanted to get up and dance because his wife had been returned to him. He probably would if he wasn't so damn tired and worried.

Kade and Travis had left for the day, but Maddie and Sam had stayed behind, Maddie hunting down the doctors to get the whole story after getting Mia's permission to do so. Thank God his sister was a physician. Max needed to hear what was happening from someone he trusted, and in a language he understood.

Sam stood and clasped his wife's hand, pulling her to her feet.

"I don't want to leave you alone here tonight, Max," Maddie said softly, her sympathetic gaze running over her brother and his disheveled appearance.

Max looked up at her, his heart warming from her sisterly concern. Putting his coffee on the table beside him, he stood up and pulled her into a bear hug. Sam plucked the coffee from his wife's hand deftly as Max swept Maddie into his arms and squeezed her tightly. "Thank you for being here when I needed you, but I'm not alone anymore. Mia's here. I'm exactly where I should be." His voice was hoarse, his emotions getting closer to the surface with exhaustion.

Releasing Maddie, he told Sam, "Take her home. She's pregnant with my nephew."

Sam snorted. "You mean my daughter?" He raised a brow at Max.

Max rolled his eyes. "My nephew," he argued good-naturedly. He knew Sam didn't care whether Maddie had a boy or girl, as long as the baby was healthy. But since he'd learned that Sam was dreaming of a little girl cousin for Simon's soon-to-arrive baby girl, Max immediately had to be contrary. It just wouldn't be natural *not* to argue with Sam.

Sam took Maddie's hand and slapped Max on the back. "Now you can have one of your own, buddy. See you tomorrow." Sam exited the waiting room with Maddie, his parting words still echoing in Max's brain.

Max had barely started to dare to believe Mia was alive, back in his life again. It was too early to start thinking about kids, but it didn't stop the longing when he thought about the fact that he might have something other than a bleak future. His heart racing, he exited the waiting room, striding quickly toward Mia's room.

His wife had been in the hospital for two days, yet he'd barely had a chance to talk to her. Someone was always taking her away for tests or exams, and when she was in her room, someone was always visiting. He wanted some time alone with her, needed it.

He didn't knock. The door was ajar and he pushed it open gently with his shoulder, his eyes immediately drawn to the bed. Max didn't know what he had been expecting, but he exhaled hard, expelling the breath of relief he hadn't realized he'd been holding. Maybe he was afraid he was delusional, or that she'd be gone. But she was there, her head down and looking at the screen of her laptop, her teeth worrying her lower lip as she tapped on the keyboard.

She's scared. I know that worried expression.

Her hair was still short, but it was blonde again, the color that she'd used apparently temporary. Most of it had washed out after the nurse had helped her shower. Max couldn't deny that he wanted to know why she had wanted to cover her blonde locks, why she'd cut her beautiful hair short, but he pushed the questions away. He wasn't getting any answers—not right now anyway. Instead, he just stared at the short curly locks that framed her beautiful face. Dressed in a pink pastel nightgown with fuzzy slippers, she looked much younger than her actual twenty-nine years.

I missed two of her birthdays. We missed two anniversaries.

No matter. Max planned on making up for every moment they'd lost. Never again would he tell himself he had time, that he had years to enjoy life with Mia *after* he'd created his empire, and especially *once he'd learned* to control the intensity of his emotions around her. The latter was the primary reason he'd focused on his business. The way he'd felt about her was too intense, too raw, too hard to hide. She'd been his one vulnerability, a major crack in his Hamilton control, and he'd had a very hard time keeping his possessive instincts in check. Now, he couldn't care less whether he was in control or not. Everything had stopped mattering to him the moment he had lost her.

Learned your lessons, dumbass?

Oh yeah, he definitely had. Life was short, and nothing really mattered except the people you cared about.

"What are you doing?" he asked curiously as he moved into the room, letting the door click closed behind him.

Her luminous blue eyes looked up from the computer, her lips curling into a happy smile as she saw him. The look was so familiar that it nearly brought him to his knees.

"Research. I'm trying to find out more about what happened to me and why I can't remember." She closed the laptop and gave him her full attention, a familiar action that had always disconcerted him and fascinated him at the same time. Now, he found it enchanting and seductive, something that helped quench a deep-seated need.

He sat in the chair next to the bed, unable to tear his eyes away from her face. "And what did you find out, Madame Detective?"

"Not much. Nothing the doctors haven't already told me. I did find it a little spooky reading about my own supposed death." She sighed and rested against the pillows behind her back before continuing, "Losing over two years of my life is scary. It seems like just yesterday that we were attending the Bannister Charity Dinner, but I can feel the hole in my life, that everything's changed." She paused and whispered softly, "I've changed."

"We'll figure it all out, sweetheart. I swear. Everything will be okay," Max answered, taking her hand in his and scooting the chair closer to the bed.

"I'm glad you're here." Her eyes moved from his face and looked at their joined hands. "Obviously I haven't been living a life of leisure. My hands are rough."

Max flipped her hand over, noticing her ragged nails and callused hands for the first time. "You've never lived a life of leisure. You're the busiest woman I know."

But her appearance was always perfect, always impeccably groomed and stylish.

The changes *were* odd, but he wasn't about to tell her that.

"Oh well. At least I'm thin," she said wistfully.

Yeah. She was. Too damn skinny. Another thing that was perplexing. Mia always had herself on some kind of diet, and Max had hated it. She'd had perfect curves, and an ass that made his cock hard every time he got a glimpse of her swaying hips in front of him. "It's nothing that some good Italian food won't fix," he told her with a grin.

She groaned. "Pasta is my enemy."

"You love it," he reminded her, wanting to laugh at a comment she'd muttered every time she'd put away a plate of fettuccini, usually followed by a healthy serving of tiramisu. Honestly, he didn't care how she looked; in his eyes, she'd always be the most beautiful woman on the planet.

She pulled her hand gently from his and set her laptop aside. Twisting her hands nervously together, she mumbled, "I had them do a DNA test. My brothers provided their blood for me to have it done. It wouldn't be as conclusive as it would be if my mom was still alive but—"

"Why? I know you're my wife. You know—"

"I want you to know for certain. I disappeared for over two years. You deserve some sort of scientific proof."

"I don't need it. I have no doubts. I knew the moment I saw you in the park, Mia," he replied, slightly annoyed that she felt she had to prove herself to him.

"I think my brother wants it," Mia said quietly, the disappointment evident in her voice.

Bastard. I'll rip his damn heart out. "Travis," Max said aloud, his tone vibrating with anger.

"No. I think Travis believes me. But I'm not so sure about Kade," Mia admitted, her expression vulnerable.

"Kade? Why the fuck does he want it?" Okay…Max could believe that Travis would want proof. He could be a coldhearted bastard who believed only in concrete facts. But Kade? "I'll kill him," he grumbled, thinking of the many ways he could torture his brother-in-law for asking this of Mia right now.

"He didn't really ask. I offered. And I think it's important that we get rid of any doubts for a lot of reasons. Kade just seems different, distant, and hesitant to accept that I'm really his sister." Mia sighed. "Maybe it's just from the disappointment of the accident and his girlfriend breaking up with him. But he seems uncertain, and I don't want anyone to have any doubts."

"I'm still fucking killing him," Max answered irritably.

"I don't think I've ever heard you drop the f-bomb before," Mia said teasingly.

"Yeah...well...things have changed. I've changed," Max admitted, knowing it was true. He wasn't the same man she had known before.

"I'm different, too. I remember our life together before I disappeared, but I don't feel like that same person anymore," she whispered just loud enough for Max to hear her. "I'm sorry."

"Hey." Max stood and tipped her chin up so he could see her gorgeous eyes. "It doesn't matter. I never stopped loving you. And I never will. We'll start over, get to know each other again." He'd take his time, let her recover, but Max was determined that Mia *would* know him.

He wanted to tell her that he knew how empty his life was without her, how his heart had bled each and every day that she'd been gone, that he wished he had died with her when he thought she was dead. But she wasn't ready for that right now, and he ruthlessly shoved the thoughts away. Right now, he just wanted her whole, healthy, and happy.

"Okay," she agreed breathlessly. "You should go home and get some rest. You look exhausted. Have you slept?"

He grinned at her. "Not much. And I'm not leaving until I can take you home tomorrow."

"You need sleep. You look tired," she murmured, worrying her lip again with distress, her expression troubled.

"I'll sleep," he assured her, hating to see her upset about him when she was the one in a hospital bed. "Here." He patted the chair next to the bed.

She hesitated before asking haltingly, "Will you sleep with me?" Scooting over in the small bed, she gave him a hopeful look.

At that moment, all Max wanted to do was slide into the bed beside her and hold her, feel her breath against his skin to remind him that she was his again. But he couldn't. "I stink. I haven't showered and I've been in the same clothes for two days."

Mia smiled and lifted her hand, pointing her thumb toward a door near the entrance of the room. "Bathroom is over there and Maddie brought you clean clothes. They're in the drawer."

Max's lips turned up as he moved to the dresser and opened the drawer, pulling out a clean pair of jeans and t-shirt, and promising himself not to forget that he owed his sister a very big favor. "Five minutes," he told Mia, practically running to the bathroom and closing the door, probably setting a world record for taking the fastest shower and still getting himself clean.

Mia was yawning when he exited the bathroom, his hair still damp, but feeling almost human again. She moved to the edge of the bed so he could slip in beside her. The bed was small and would have been tight for a man his size even without another body, but at the moment, it was heaven. Pulling Mia away from the edge of the bed to cradle her back against his front, he groaned with ecstasy as her scent surrounded him, happily drowning him in her essence. His heart thundered, his body reveling in a sensation he thought he'd never experience again.

"Jesus. I missed this so much," he whispered huskily against her ear, his hand reaching up to swipe the string that turned off the light above them, plunging them into darkness.

Mia relaxed into his body, fitting perfectly against him. "I don't remember us *not* being together, but I know that I missed it too. I love you," she said in a quiet, solemn voice.

His whole body shuddered as his hold on her tightened involuntarily. His hand splayed over her stomach, urging her closer. Those were the words he'd wanted to hear, needed to hear. As long as Mia loved him, not another damn thing in the world mattered. "I love you, too. I didn't think I'd ever get to hold you again." His voice was choked, emotion lodging in his throat.

"I'm not sure my nurse will approve," she said with a light laugh.

"Don't give a fuck," he murmured against her ear, breathing in the scent of her hair. "Are you comfortable?"

"Yes. You smell so good," she said in a sultry voice. "Are you okay?"

"Hell, no. Hospital beds are like torture devices. But you couldn't blast me out of this position with dynamite right now," he told her honestly. "And I owe Maddie a hell of a nice present for the clean clothes."

"She's wonderful, Max. I'm so happy you found each other. How did it happen?" she asked curiously.

He shrugged slightly as he replied, "Fate. Or maybe just dumb luck. I saw her at Simon's wedding to Kara and she looked just like an old picture of our birth mother. It made me want to dig into my past and I finally found the proof that we were brother and sister. Unfortunately, she didn't get adopted and she's had it pretty tough. I wish I had known earlier. I was just a baby when we were separated and neither one of us remembered the other."

"She seems happy now," Mia mused.

"She is. How could she not be? She has me for a brother," Max answered with a chuckle.

"I know she's happy to have you as a brother, but I sort of think Sam has a little bit to do with it too," Mia answered with a sigh. "They look so happy. Maddie told me some of their story. I never thought Sam would become so domesticated. I guess underneath the playboy exterior, he was always yearning for Maddie. I guess both Simon and Sam are finally happy. It seems so strange that everything has changed so much. It's almost like I went to sleep one night and woke up to an alternate universe. But I'm glad both of them found the right woman. I'm glad. I always worried about them. I wish that would happen for Kade and Travis."

Max was pissed as hell at Kade, and Travis needed a woman who'd grab him by the balls and wouldn't let go, because he could be an asshole, but Max answered magnanimously, "I hope so, too." And he did, because that's what Mia wanted. Kade could find the right woman to please Mia...right after Max beat the hell out of him for being an asshole.

"Will you stay for a while? Until I remember or at least get used to the fact that I don't remember the last few years?" Her voice sounded nervous, frightened. "Everything just seems so dissimilar to what I can remember."

"Sweetheart, I'm staying all night," he reminded her.

She shook her head slightly. "That's not what I meant. I was wondering if you could put off your business trips. Just for a little while. The media will have a field day with this, and I was hoping you might be able to stick around for a while."

Guilt made Max's body tense and his gut burn. "Mia, I'm not going anywhere."

"What about work, your plan to conquer the business and political world?" she questioned, her voice confused.

Yeah, at one time he had wanted to run for political office, but those desires had completely fled. He'd wanted it for all the wrong reasons, and he'd discovered he would make a lousy politician. "I told you I've changed. I don't want the same things as I wanted back then." He released a masculine sigh as he continued, "And I've conquered everything I want to conquer in the business world. I don't need to travel like that anymore." Actually, most of the trips hadn't been critical, but he didn't want to think about that right now. "I'm afraid you're stuck with me."

"It will be nice to have you home," Mia said with a yawn. "I miss you so much when you're gone. I need you to help me get used to all the changes that have happened. I wish my memory would just come back."

Max could have told her that he understood the loneliness she had felt, but he doubted that she could handle exactly how much he'd missed her—during their marriage when he traveled a lot, and during the years she had been taken away from him.

"You won't have a chance to even miss me," he informed her playfully. In a sterner voice he told her, "You're also going to be surrounded by security from this day forward. No arguments. No more going around unsecured. No more ducking our security. You're being protected. Always."

"I know I ought to disagree, but I won't. Not now. I'm actually relieved," she admitted, her voice sounding lost in the dark.

"And you aren't going to be exposed to the media either," he rumbled adamantly. "I'll make a brief statement when the media finds out, and that's all they're getting."

"I'd rather avoid them for now. At least until I remember what happened." Mia shifted position slightly, rubbing against him as she moved, her ass flexing against his groin. "Max, are you…" Her voice trailed off, her question unfinished.

He knew exactly what she was going to ask. "Am I hard? Yep. My cock is like granite right now. Everything about you arouses me, and I've been without for over two years, sweetheart. So you need to quit squirming against me like that," he answered. "Be still."

Her body stopped shifting, but she asked curiously, "You didn't… you never…nobody ever…" She stopped and then continued, "You didn't sleep with anyone while I was gone?"

"Nope. And I didn't fuck anyone either. I had no desire to screw a woman who wasn't you," he answered bluntly.

"But didn't you ever want to—"

"The only thing I wanted was my wife. So I got myself off thinking of you, because there was no one else I wanted." Max figured if they were starting again, he might as well get honest. He and Mia had never discussed sexual things this bluntly, but maybe they should have. "Does that surprise you?"

She was silent for a moment, so quiet that Max thought she had fallen asleep before she answered. "Actually, the thought of you doing that is pretty hot." Her voice was low, husky, with a fuck-me-right-now vibe running through her words that he'd never heard before and nearly made him groan with frustrated lust. "I wish I could have watched," she added quietly, almost as though she was talking to herself.

Her comment was candid, straightforward, and as blunt as his had been. Max didn't think it was possible for his cock to get any stiffer, but it did. It was doing some major expansion underneath the denim of his jeans, straining the seams. They had never really flirted or engaged in sexual banter quite this blunt, and doing so now was making his whole body burn. "Go to sleep and behave yourself," he ordered, his cock twitching in disagreement with that idea.

"Okay. Promise you'll stay?"

It nearly killed him that she even had to ask again, but considering how he had handled things in the past, he shouldn't be surprised. "I promise."

Max lay awake in the dark, listening to Mia's breathing as it evened out and got deeper. Her body went completely pliant in his arms, and he willed himself to relax.

He thought he'd never fall asleep in his uncomfortable, cramped position, but he did. And it ended up being the most restful and peaceful slumber he'd had in a very long time.

Chapter 3

"Aren't you ever going to stop looking and buy something?" Max commented with a smile in his voice, matching his stride to hers as they walked hand in hand around the mall. "You've been looking for over an hour."

Mia had been out of the hospital for two days, wandering around their enormous home feeling lost and wondering what she really *should* be doing. She was a jewelry designer and she had a workshop at home, but Max had insisted she relax and not try to push herself to start working right away. Going into her workshop felt somehow "off" to her, uncomfortable, so she wasn't feeling creative anyway. There was very little for her to do except try to figure out exactly why she felt so differently, what had happened to cause the enormous black hole she felt stretching into a huge void in her past. Everything was the same, yet *she* was so very different. One moment it seemed as if her married life with Max had never been interrupted, but at other times, it seemed as if there was a huge gulf between the two of them, and she could truly feel how much time had passed, how much they had both changed.

She glanced up at Max and smiled back at him, her breath hitching as she looked at him, dressed casually in a pair of jeans and a t-shirt, so masculine and so damn perfect that she wanted to just stand still and drink him in.

That's one thing that hasn't changed. I can still hardly breathe whenever I'm near him.

"Everything's so expensive here," she answered, wondering when she'd begun worrying about prices.

"I think I can afford it," Max replied with a bark of laughter.

Mia sighed as she absorbed the sound of his laughter, something that had always made her heart skitter. Except now it seemed to make her pulse pound like a jackhammer. Somehow, every moment with Max was so much more intense now, more important. Not that her feelings for him hadn't always been powerful, and she'd always known that her love for him was much fiercer than the way he felt about her. Oh, she knew he loved her, but Max was almost an obsession for her, a crazy love that she knew she'd never get over. Max was…well…he was Max, and he did nothing to extremes.

She shrugged as she answered him. "It just seems ridiculous to pay hundreds for a pair of jeans. Why?"

"Why, why, why? You're still the most inquisitive female I've ever known and I think that's still your favorite word." His eyes were covetous and adoring as they swept over her, amusement in their depths.

"It just doesn't make sense," she said defensively, wondering if he disliked the changes in her personality. She didn't know where some of them were coming from; she just felt…peculiar, like two different women in the same body.

Max stopped and nudged her to the side of the mall traffic. Her ass hit the wall gently as he asked curiously, "What happened to the woman who bought her clothing without even checking the price tag?" He put one palm against the wall beside her head and tipped her chin up to look at him. "I'm wealthy, Mia. Incredibly wealthy. And for that matter, so are you. Your grandmother's trust has done nothing but grow since you've been gone. You never touched a penny of it."

Mia shook her head, confused. "I know that. I don't know why I feel the way I do. I know how I used to feel, and it was me; it was who I was. Now I don't know who I am anymore." She had to blink to keep the tears from falling, feeling hopeless, like she'd never find the woman who Max loved again. "I feel like I should pretend to be the way I was before because you loved me that way."

"I. Still. Love. You," Max answered gruffly, the muscles in his jaw twitching and his eyes growing stormy. "Do you think I give a fuck about your shopping habits?"

Mia stared up at him, unable to tear her eyes away from his volatile expression. He looked raw and hungry, feral and dangerous. Fascinated, she watched his beautiful hazel eyes radiate with a fiery intensity she'd never seen before on the face of the man she loved. She might not feel like the woman Max had fallen in love with, but Max had changed too. She'd noticed the difference. Problem was, he was even hotter than he'd ever been.

"You dropped the f-bomb again," she babbled, unable to think of anything else to say. Her core flooded with heat. All she wanted was for him to touch her, the need almost unbearable. Max had always been an incredible, unselfish, tender lover, always bringing her to climax before he satisfied himself. But she'd never seen him like this: he was starving and she was the only prey he wanted to devour.

He leaned in closer, so close she could feel his heated breath on her cheek. "Does my cursing bother you?" he asked in a low, husky voice against her ear, making her shiver.

"No," she answered honestly. Really, the way he said it made her whole body catch fire, and her mind wander to images of him not only saying the word, but doing it to her. He hadn't touched her in a sexual way in the two days she'd been home, and she had been starting to think he didn't desire her anymore, that her slimmer body, short hair, rougher appearance, and different personality turned him off.

"Good. Then I don't give a fuck," he whispered against her lips before his mouth closed over hers with a force that made her gasp into his mouth as he took it.

Max didn't kiss—he ravaged—and Mia moaned as his mouth conquered hers, winding her arms around his neck to stay on her feet as her knees turned to water and her whole body quivered. She speared her fingers through his short hair, engulfed in a passion so fierce that she wanted to wrap her legs around his waist and let him take her right here, right now. He was all barely-leashed masculine power and dominance, and she was more than willing to submit, to experience more of this raw and uninhibited Max.

One hand cradled the back of her head to keep it from slamming against the wall, while the other cupped her ass, yanking her core closer to his groin. His tongue was relentless, entering and retreating, mimicking the act that she so desperately wanted.

She whimpered as Max jerked his mouth from hers, his breath harsh and audible against her ear. "Shit. We're in the middle of a goddamn mall and I'm ready to tear your clothes off and fuck you blind." And he didn't sound happy about it.

"I didn't think you wanted to anymore," Mia admitted softly, still stunned.

"Oh, I want to. You have no idea the things I want to do to you. I'm just not sure you're ready for it. I told you I've changed, Mia. And I'm not sure I can control myself anymore." He yanked his head back and speared her with tortured eyes.

She ran her hand along his cheek, loving the abrasive texture of his five o'clock shadow against her fingers. "Then don't." *Sweet Jesus*...if what had just happened was what was in store for her now, she'd take the raw and rough version of Max exactly the way he was, and she'd wallow in him. This was a man who could get down and dirty, and she wanted that more than she ever imagined she would. "I need you."

Mia watched his face as he struggled with himself. She could sense his hesitation, but if the animalistic expression she saw was any indication, the desire to fuck her was winning.

He grabbed her hand and pulled her back into the mall foot traffic. "I'm losing it," he mumbled, leading her into a trendy, moderately priced store. "Find some stuff. Walk away, Mia, before I embarrass both of us," he ordered quietly but firmly as he let go of her hand and flopped into a chair near the door.

Mia knew he wanted distance, but she was reluctant to give it to him. She didn't want him to gain control. What she really wanted was to explore this different Max, find out how hot he could really burn, but they were in a mall with a gazillion people around and he'd already embarrassed himself by kissing her breathless against a wall.

I wanted him so desperately that I didn't care. I would let him take me anywhere he wanted because I forget everything when he kisses me.

Her face started to turn pink as she watched his security agents who had been following them seat themselves in other available chairs by the door.

Oh God, I forgot about them. I forgot about everybody. I was too consumed by Max.

No doubt the agents had probably turned their backs and shielded her and Max from view, but it was still a little mortifying to remember that they were being tailed—and watched—as she and Max were groping each other in a public mall.

And we're trying to avoid media attention? Way to go, Mia. Excellent way to avoid detection. No wonder Max was trying to get a grip on himself.

Making her way to the casual clothing, Mia selected several pair of jeans and shirts, forcing herself not to look at the price tag this time. She needed to get some clothing that fit. Max hadn't moved a thing in their house, and she still had her old clothes, but most of them were baggy, her body at least a size smaller. Frowning as she gathered what she wanted, she admitted to herself that she'd probably be able to wear them again in no time. Max was feeding her constantly, like he was trying to make up for some kind of deprivation. Obviously, she hadn't been deprived. She was slender, but definitely not starving.

Max met her at the checkout, silently handing the clerk his platinum credit card, his mood unreadable.

Mia reached for her bags, but Max beat her to it after retrieving his card, grabbing the bags in one arm and taking her hand in his, squeezing it gently as they left the store.

"Are you upset about what happened? I know you hate undignified displays of affection in public," she asked curiously as they strolled toward the main entrance of the mall.

"Hell no, I'm not upset. I'm pissed off," he answered bluntly.

"Why?" Mia asked, surprised. Max rarely got angry.

"Because I couldn't finish what I started," he grumbled, but his tone was slightly amused. "You have no idea how close you just came to being fucked up against a wall by your desperate husband."

"There was always the dressing room," she contemplated, teasing him now. Having Max want her this badly was like a potent aphrodisiac that made her body ache to have him inside her. Anyplace. Anywhere. Anytime.

Max shot her a disgruntled look as he held the exit door open for her to walk outside. "Now you tell me."

"Would you have done it?" she asked curiously, fascinated by her own husband's desire for her.

"In a heartbeat, had I thought of it," he told her huskily, need radiating in his voice. Taking her hand in his, he started walking toward the car, his security following at a distance behind them.

"We couldn't have done that anyway," Mia said regretfully. "Unless you're carrying a condom in your pocket."

Max shot her a perplexed gaze. "Why? We've never needed one before."

Mia looked down at the pavement, shame burning her cheeks. "Because we don't know what happened to me, Max. You have no idea what could have happened."

"Are you afraid you were unfaithful?" Max asked huskily and hesitantly.

"No," she murmured. "Whatever happened, I know myself, maybe better than I ever did before, and I never had thoughts about being with any other man but you. I love you the same way you love me. But we don't know if I was abducted or…" Mia had a hard time saying the last word, but she spit it out, "raped. I can't put you at risk, Max. Not until I know for sure exactly what happened. I'll see my doctor and get a check-up, but I need to regain my memory."

Max tugged at her hand, stopping her beside his vehicle. "You will. Sweetheart, you know if something did happen, I'll kill whoever did it. And it won't make a bit of difference in how I feel about you. Tell me you know that." His eyes were pleading and tormented.

"If it happened, it wasn't by choice," she said, her voice choked with emotion. "I love you, Max. So very much it hurts. It makes my skin crawl just thinking about being with anyone else."

Max tipped her chin up to look at him, his eyes blazing with emotion. "You'll be with me."

"I can't." God, her heart ached for him. *I need to remember.*

"I'll empty every drugstore in Tampa and the surrounding area of their condom supply," he told her sincerely, giving her a lopsided grin that made her heart surge.

He was trying to take her mind off what she might have experienced, trying to draw her back into something happier…and it worked. Max was irresistible when he was playing with her, and it used to happen so seldom. She was mush in the face of his wicked grin. "Kind of ambitious, don't you think?"

"Not at all," he told her arrogantly. "I'm thinking I might need more flown in from other cities."

Oh God, she loved this man, and she loved the way he loved her now. Or the way he must have always loved her, but had never shown it until recently. "Thinking about finishing what we started in the mall?"

"Yeah. And then starting it all over again," he answered, his voice graveled, low, and sensually potent.

Remembering Max's dominant, uncontrolled embrace, Mia blurted out, "Later. You can definitely finish it later."

"Count on it," Max said, his tone low and dangerous.

Mia's core clenched, her already damp panties getting wetter. Max had always been a man of his word. If he said something, he meant it. He might be different, but Mia knew that was one thing that would never change.

Thank God!

"I can't find my wedding ring. I've searched everywhere," Mia murmured quietly as she and Max were eating supper that evening. Max had arranged dinner at home, Italian food from her favorite restaurant.

"You had to have been wearing it when you disappeared. It's never been here," Max answered, looking up at her as he dropped the fork on his empty plate.

Mia could see the hurt look in his eyes, and it almost leveled her. Obviously he'd noticed it was missing, but he hadn't said anything. "Why would I take it off if I was wearing it? I never took it off."

"I know," he answered grimly. "I wondered about that myself."

Frustrated, Mia dropped her napkin on her empty plate and reached for her glass of wine. She took a sip, trying desperately to remember what had happened, to conjure memories, any information about the past few years. As usual, she could see nothing but a blank space of time, as though she'd been sleeping through the last few years. "I can't remember," she admitted softly, wanting desperately to know what had happened. She needed to know, and so did Max. Obviously the uncertainty was haunting both of them. "Tell me what happened after I disappeared. Were there ever any clues to where I went, what I did?"

"No," Max replied darkly. "The last thing you remember happened a week or two before you disappeared." He stopped and reached for his beer, taking a gulp before he continued, "I'm not even completely sure what day you vanished. I found your things on the beach the day I came home from an overnight business trip. It could have been the day I left or the following day. I came home late. I hated myself for ever leaving on that trip."

He looked tormented, and she hated it. "Max, it wasn't your fault. You were considering running for public office, and you had business out of town—"

"It was bullshit. All of it. I never wanted to be a politician, and I could have left most of the traveling to upper management. I was a goddamn coward, Mia. I took those trips to take a break from us." After downing the rest of his beer, he stood abruptly and went to the refrigerator for another one.

Mia felt her hand trembling as she reached for her wine, taking a healthy sip. He needed a break? Had he wanted out of their marriage? "Was I suffocating you because I loved you too much?" It was a hard question to ask, but she needed to know. Max had been her whole world since they'd met, and maybe it was too much for him. She had a tendency to be a bit extreme in everything she did, while Max was exactly the opposite. Maybe he couldn't bear her intensity for long periods of time, even though she'd really tried to tone it down for his sake, not wanting to scare him away.

Max twisted the top off his beer, laughing harshly as he tossed the cap in the trash. "It wasn't you; it was me. I wanted to be smothered by you; I wanted to be the only man you saw, the only man who existed for you."

"But Max, you *were*—"

"It wasn't enough," he told her roughly as he slid into his chair again, piercing her with a possessive stare that Mia had never seen before. "The things I wanted weren't right in my mind. My dad loved my mom and treated her with tenderness and devotion. Although I felt those things too, there was also this total obsession that I didn't think was right, natural. You're my wife, a woman who deserves my respect. I never wanted you to leave me. I didn't want to scare you away by acting like a lunatic. The way I felt wasn't rational. I wanted to kill any man who looked at you."

Oh, God. He'd felt the same way she did, and he hadn't been able to deal with it. The crazy love, the over-the-top desire to rip his clothes off and have wild, crazy sex until they were both so sated they couldn't move. Her levelheaded Max, her sensible husband, her tender lover really felt the same savage emotions. He just hadn't wanted her to know.

"So you're really a closet dominant male?" she asked, shivering as she watched his face, the turbulent emotions making the flecks of gold in his eyes glow as he stared at her as though he wanted to swallow her whole. Her core flooded with heat as she watched him struggle, secretly hoping the alpha would break free. Just once... she'd like to see Max totally lose control, not in a bad way, but in a very, very good way. It would make him more human, more real, and she welcomed it.

If that's a part of Max I haven't seen...bring it on!

"I think I'm beyond that, and I don't think I'm in the closet anymore. And I'm still perfectly rational with everyone and everything except you. You're the only woman who's ever made me feel this way," he growled, his face damp with perspiration.

Mia tried to hide the longing that she was certain was showing on her face, wanting to do nothing except crawl into his lap and make him completely lose control. The feminine power she had over him was suddenly a heady, dizzying feeling. This man, who was her entire world, wanted her above all things, above any other woman on earth, and she knew she could make him lose it. But he had trusted her with his feelings, and she wasn't going to use them against him when he was struggling, vulnerable. She loved him too much. What he'd been taught growing up by the parents he'd loved and the way he was feeling now were warring against each other.

Everything inside of her rejoiced, elated to know that he'd felt the same as she did, that his love was anything but lukewarm and tepid, controlled and sane. Now, it seemed almost ridiculous that they had both never fully revealed the intensity of their emotions for fear of losing the one they loved to the point of insanity. "You can be whoever you really are with me, Max. I'll never stop loving you."

"I think that's the problem. I was never truly alive until I met you. I was the guy who never lost his temper, never let emotions get in the way of a business deal, and I was pretty much indifferent about everything. The only thing I wanted was to be a good son to my adoptive parents because they had given me so much. I guess I thought I needed to be in their image, act like a Hamilton, to make up for the fact that I wasn't their blood child. I didn't even know who I was," Max admitted.

"And do you know who you are now?" Mia asked softly, loving him even more for being able to bare himself to her.

"Not completely," he said with a masculine sigh. "But I can guarantee you that I'm not indifferent, especially not when it comes to you. I know exactly how I feel about you. I always have. I just wasn't sure you could handle it."

"I can," she told him emphatically. Trying to give him a reprieve, she glanced away from him and asked calmly, "Tell me what happened after you found out I was missing."

Max took a deep breath before he answered, "Obviously, there was an extensive search, but it only lasted about a week because there were no leads. After that, they were convinced you had either drowned or there was only one possible suspect if you were murdered. They weren't really looking at other possibilities because nothing else made sense."

"Who?" she asked him, confused.

"Me," he answered, his voice low and hoarse. "A woman with no real enemies vanishes and can't be found, the usual suspect is her husband."

"Oh, God. Max, I'm so sorry." It had to have been awful for him, being suspected of murdering his own wife. "There was no motive, no reason to even suspect you."

Max shrugged. "Crime of passion? Another woman? Another man? Money? Believe me…they checked every possibility, dug through every record to make sure I hadn't done anything to you for any of those reasons. When they finally decided I wasn't guilty, they assumed you had drowned. They said they didn't suspect foul play. There was never a demand for ransom, no reason to believe you were abducted. There was no activity on any of your accounts. It was like you had just…vanished."

Tears sprung to Mia's eyes as she watched him trying so hard to impersonally state just the facts when he'd so obviously suffered.

Had their positions been reversed, she wasn't sure she could have come out of it still sane. "The media must have been horrible."

"Luckily I was spared that part of it. They kept the investigation quiet. I cooperated, gave them whatever they wanted."

Whatever she had done, Mia hated herself for putting Max through hell. He was a man with pride, a man of integrity, and being stripped of all that he was for the investigation had to have been devastating. Squeezing her eyes closed to prevent her tears from falling, she whispered softly, "I wish I could remember. I wish I knew why I did this to you."

Max rose from his chair and scooped her up, sitting back down in her chair with her cradled in his lap. "Hey, don't cry. You don't know what your reason was or what happened. Don't blame yourself. I survived. You're here now. That's all that matters to me."

Opening her eyes, the tears falling down her cheeks, she asked him, "Why are you still wearing your ring? You must have given up hope, thought I was dead." She lifted his hand, running a finger over the platinum band and feeling lost without her own wedding ring. Sure... it was just an object, but it was a symbol of her love for Max, and she missed the heavy weight on her finger. Her wedding day had been the happiest day of her life, and the loss of her ring nearly killed her.

Spearing his hand into her hair, he tilted her head back as he told her roughly, "I never gave up hope. Right after you disappeared, I made a promise to you that I'd never give up. I couldn't. In my heart, I never accepted that you were dead. I guess I thought that if you really were, I would feel it."

A sob escaped Mia's lips as she looked at Max's earnest, fierce expression.

Why? What possible reason could I have had to put him through this?

She could remember their life together up until a week or so before she'd disappeared. Granted, they had both been hiding, afraid to reveal some parts of themselves. But they had loved each other, and there had never, not once, been any thoughts of betraying or leaving Max for any reason.

Clutching at his shirt, fisting handfuls of it as she cried, she managed to tell him in an anguished voice, "I want to remember. I have to know why."

Max grasped both of her wrists and wrapped them around his neck. His actions were gentle, but his voice was stern. "Stop it, Mia. Stop doing this to yourself. You'll remember and everything will be fine."

She shuddered as the fight left her body, her emotions spent, her head dropping onto his broad shoulder. Her mouth was close to the bare skin of his neck and she inhaled deeply, letting the masculine, sexy musk of him surround her. At the moment, she was safe in Max's arms. Unfortunately, for some reason, she didn't completely share his optimism. Some warning, some niggling sixth sense was telling her that even though she needed to remember, things wouldn't be all right. Something was wrong. Horribly wrong. She just hoped that when the hole in her memory was filled, the knowledge wouldn't destroy them both.

Two women in the same body. All she could hope for now was to figure out who she really was, and which one was the real Mia.

Chapter 4

Mia stopped her descent down the elegant staircase of her home, a towel and blanket in her hand, to listen to the powerful music coming from their grand piano. Although she identified the skilled fingers of Max immediately, the violence of the music grabbed hold of her, halting her progress down the stairs just to listen.

Max had always been an accomplished pianist, sometimes playing the works of the Masters, but occasionally working on a composition of his own. This one was definitely nothing she recognized, and she knew instinctively it was his own work. The melody went from hauntingly, achingly beautiful, and then transforming into a violent crescendo, building until nearly her entire body was trembling from the intensity of the music. Sitting, her ass hit one of the steps; her hand grasped one of the wooden balusters and she rested her head against the oak banister, tears filling her eyes as her husband poured his soul into his music. Mia could feel every emotion: love, frustration, loneliness, hopelessness, desperation. They all mixed and swirled, wringing the same emotions from her heart that he was feeling with his music.

Tucker plopped down next to her, resting his head in her lap. Mia stroked him absently, loving the feel of her canine companion. "Something's not right, Tucker," she whispered, wishing the dog could talk. Tucker had always had a strange instinct, as though he knew when something was wrong. He was trying to comfort her now, and she rubbed his belly, feeling better just because he was her comrade. "Has he been playing like this while I was gone?" she asked the dog softly, smiling as Tucker gave her a doggy look of understanding.

Max and Tucker had bonded, and although her dog still came to her for his daily dose of affection, he seemed to be loyal to Max now too. Rolling his pudgy body back into sitting position, the canine gave her a questioning look.

"Go to him," she urged the dog, knowing Tucker was torn between her and Max, both of them confused and in need of his company.

With a final doggie lick to her hand, Tucker waddled down the stairs and toward the music room. Mia knew from watching her man and her dog together that Tucker would plop down at Max's feet, not expecting a massive amount of affection from Max. But Tucker seemed content just to share space with the man who had fed, watered, and cared for him for the last few years.

The piece stopped with a final discordant note, the silence followed by fingers toying with the keys. Mia took a deep breath and released it, stunned by the volatile composition. Max usually played with consummate skill, making a piano sing, but she'd never felt so much emotion pulsating through his music.

Suddenly, she realized she'd never really done much else except scratch the surface of Max's emotions. He was always so controlled and sensible in every aspect of his life. She'd never looked deeper, afraid that she wouldn't see what she so desperately needed to find.

She stood and made her way to the French doors off the dining room, slipping out just as Max started playing Mozart, his playing controlled again, and absolutely perfect.

She sighed as the warm, humid air hit her scantily-clad body. She'd dug up an old bikini and donned it, throwing on one of Max's t-shirts over the top. The water was beckoning, and she took the wooden stairs to the beach two at a time, eager to feel the water caressing her skin, turning on the porch light as she went. It was dark, but between the moon, stars, and the dim light from the porch, her favorite spot in the world was transformed into a dimly lit paradise. Spreading the blanket, she breathed in the sea air. She'd wanted to ask Max to come with her, but they had separated after dinner. He'd gone to his music room and she'd gone upstairs to do another search for her wedding ring—an unsuccessful endeavor that had left her depressed and confused. Had it been stolen, taken away from her? There was no other way anyone would have gotten it off her finger. She'd needed to relax, to try to forget for just a little while how much her life had changed and deal with the huge hole in her existence.

Lifting the shirt from her body and dropping it on the sand, she headed for the water, trying to leave her jumbled thoughts behind her.

The moment Max realized that Mia wasn't in the house...he panicked. He'd gone upstairs to find her, but she was nowhere to be found.

"Mia," he bellowed, checking every room downstairs as he called her name. "She's here somewhere. She has to be here," he chanted in a whisper to himself as every room came up empty.

Entering the dining room, he saw the porch light on and the door ajar. "No. Fuck no," he said in a husky, desperate voice. Kicking the door open, his eyes scanned the beach from the porch, and what he saw sent his heart into palpitations. Perspiration formed on his face as he leaped down the stairs, sprinting across the sand. "No, goddammit. No."

He saw her head go under the water, and he dove into the waves, not caring that he was fully clothed. The denim of his jeans slowed him down, but his horror and fear had him swimming toward her like a madman. Her head popped up beside him, and he snaked his arm around her waist.

He heard her scream, not recognizing him until she'd swiped the water from her eyes. "Max. Shit. You scared the hell out of me." She tried to break his grip, but he didn't let go, treading water as he kept her firmly in his grasp.

"Get out of the water," he growled at her, his whole body shuddering as he pushed her toward shore. "Now!"

He pushed her in front of him, shoving her back toward shore. She sputtered as she started swimming. "I'm close to shore. The water is barely over my head," she shouted as she swam steadily toward the sandy beach.

"Move." The command was sharp, and Max didn't give a shit. He wanted her out of the water, back on shore, somewhere safe. Damn it. Didn't she realize she couldn't swim at night or alone? Not ever. He'd just gotten her back and he wasn't losing her again. He despised this beach, and he hadn't set foot on it again after he'd spent the night here over two years ago, shedding tears for the first time and only time, and waking up to the knowledge that his wife could very well be gone from his life forever. He hated this damn place. He hated the sand, the water, the memories of thinking this was the last place that Mia had been before she'd died.

The moment she stood, Max swept her up into his arms and carried her to the blanket on the beach. He laid her down and came down on top of her, breathless, more from his dread and horror of seeing her in the water than from exertion. He wanted—no, he needed—her compliance. He didn't care if he couldn't hide his emotions anymore. Having her under him, at his mercy, was exactly what he needed, and he reveled in it. Adrenaline was still pounding through his body as he trapped her hands over her head, urging him to take what was his, what belonged to him.

"Mine." His voice was feral and animalistic, his cock pressing against the saturated denim of his jeans.

The light was dim, but he could still see her face, and she didn't look the least bit frightened. She looked at him with longing, aroused, and it nudged him even closer to insanity just knowing she wanted him this way. She didn't struggle...she relaxed, yielding to him so sweetly that it was his undoing, making every possessive and dominant instinct he'd been holding back since the moment he'd met her explode from his body like they had been spring loaded, as if the button to release had finally been pushed, and there was no way those emotions would ever go back inside him again.

Max Hamilton had finally lost his famous Hamilton restraint, and it felt fucking fantastic.

"Max?" Mia whispered, watching the turbulent emotions that raced over the face of the man above her, and God help her, he was smoking hot. Her core had flooded with heat as he'd claimed her with one word, his feral expression warning her that he was ready to make good on everything he'd said earlier.

"You'll never set foot on this beach again. Never. I fucking hate this place," he said vehemently, water still dripping from his face and hair, his expression fierce, his breath sawing in and out of his lungs so quickly that he looked like he was gasping for air.

Mia didn't doubt what had set off his reaction. This was the beach of her supposed demise. He was freaking out about her. But she loved this beach and she wasn't going to make promises she couldn't keep. "I'll make sure someone else is here. I promise. You know I love it here," she pleaded.

"I hate it," he retorted sharply.

Fine. Then she'd make it a better memory, starting now. "Let me go. Let me touch you," she whispered softly.

"No. I'm going to fuck you here. Right here. Right now." He leaned forward and told her in a husky voice near her ear, "I'm going to taste you first until you beg for my cock, and then I'll fuck you until you beg for mercy, sweetheart."

Holy shit. She was ready to beg right now. Her cool, controlled Max was ready to get down and dirty. And talk that way, too. It made her question everything she knew about Max, how well she had really known her own husband. He was disciplined and composed, even in his lovemaking. But he didn't look the least bit restrained now. He looked ravenous, savage, all of his ferocity completely concentrated on her. "Condom," she reminded him. "We need to get some."

Reaching into the pocket of his soggy jeans, he yanked out a handful of condoms, saved from the water by plastic wrap and dropped them on the sand. "It was my first goddamn priority," he rasped.

Her pussy still quivered from his naughty taunts, and she was unable to stop herself from answering, "Good. Then fuck me. And make me come," she dared him, somehow knowing exactly what to say to push his buttons.

That wasn't something she'd normally say, but it felt good to say it now. She had never cursed or talked dirty during their marriage because Max hadn't, but she didn't seem to have that problem anymore.

Two women in the same body…again.

"Sweetheart, there's no question about whether or not you'll come. You will…and you'll be screaming my name while you're doing it," he promised dangerously.

Mia stared up at his ferocious expression, knowing that she should probably try to rein him in. He was reacting to fear and anxiety, her disappearance making him act out of character. But God…she wanted him this way. He was raw, masculine, and dangerous: a different side of Max that she had never known existed beneath his smooth exterior. And he was completely irresistible. She wasn't the least bit afraid of him. Max would never harm her. In fact, she was so aroused that her whole body was burning white-hot, so ready for him that she needed him inside her this very moment. "I'm not a screamer," she reminded him casually, although her emotions were rampant.

"You will be," he replied, his voice so husky and determined that it shot straight to Mia's gut, vibrating down to settle between her quivering thighs. "Don't move," he demanded as he released her wrists and jerked his sodden t-shirt over his head, revealing an incredible body that hadn't changed much in the last few years. Max Hamilton had a hot body that was often hidden under a suit and tie, every bit of muscle well-defined and sleek from his daily work-outs, making her want to lick every inch of his muscular chest and defined abs. And then she wanted to follow that little happy trail of hair from his belly button that tantalizingly disappeared into the waistband of his jeans.

She wasn't a screamer; she'd worried that Max might be repulsed by her base reaction to his lovemaking. She'd always tried hard to be the elegant woman she thought Max wanted as a partner, a woman he would be proud to be married to. Slowly, she'd changed herself to be the woman she'd thought he wanted and needed, trying to give up her often times impulsive behavior to make him happier. She hadn't quite gotten there yet, but she had been working at it. At least…she had…before she'd disappeared.

"Y-you actually want me to scream," she stuttered, suddenly confused by this Max she didn't know, but totally intrigued her.

Grabbing the cups of the top of her bathing suit, he broke the string between them easily, baring her breasts to the balmy night air. Her nipples were hard and sensitive, aching for his touch, and she moaned as he cupped her breasts in his hands, circling her nipples with his thumbs.

"Oh hell, yeah. Scream, moan, beg, come for me," he demanded harshly, his face intense as he watched his hands run over her breasts, over and over again. "I want to hear you."

"We're outside," she told him, panting with each stroke to her hardened nipples.

"You want me to stop?" he asked gently as he moved back, straddling her thighs, and lowering his head to her breast.

One touch of his lips, one stroke of his tongue, and she was completely lost. "No. Please." Her arms moved involuntarily, her hands fisting in his hair. "I need you, Max. Now."

"You're so beautiful," he groaned against her breast as he nipped and sucked on one nipple and teased the other with his fingers. "You belong to me, Mia. You always have," he told her roughly as his mouth moved from her breast to her abdomen, licking a trail of fire down her belly.

Ready to cry with frustration, she sighed when he broke the ties that held the back and front of her bikini bottom together, parted her legs and slid between them, his tongue still placing decadent licks on her lower abdomen.

One swipe of his powerful arm yanked the bottom of the bikini away from her, throwing it away to land somewhere on the beach, the strings broken. Mia held her breath as his fingers skimmed over the neatly trimmed hair on her pussy, so different from before, when she'd gone for Brazilian waxing, a procedure that she'd always found to be akin to female torture. Obviously, whatever she had done, she hadn't kept up the habit, instead settling for trimming and shaving.

"This is mine. So feminine. So sweet. So delicious," he rumbled, his mouth already nuzzling against her folds.

Her breath left her lungs in a long moan, the feel of his lips on her trembling flesh and his searing tongue parting her folds completely destroying her. She was beyond caring about anything but that talented tongue, and she needed it on her throbbing clit more than she needed her next breath. "Oh God, please Max. Please."

He opened her legs wider, spreading her out like a feast. And he gorged, leaving liquid fire wherever his tongue touched, making her entire body quiver as he devoured her. There was none of his gentle, slowly inflaming technique involved. His hunger was insatiable and he tasted her like a starving man who couldn't stop himself from jumping on his food once he'd found it.

He laid siege to her clit, diving through her drenched folds to run his tongue around and over the enflamed bud, groaning as he slipped two fingers into her clenching channel. Her internal muscles pulled tightly around them, trying to hold them there and her hips lifted to take in more. More. She needed more. "Max. Please."

She was needy and desperate, so ready for Max to take her. "Fuck me, Max. Please."

She couldn't take another moment of his teasing tongue and marauding fingers that were now curling and stroking her sweet spot as he teased her mercilessly. It wasn't like he'd never went down on her before...but dear God...not like this, not like a man with a mission:

bold, determined, and completely wild. It was usually foreplay, a tool he used to get her aroused and ready. But not this time.

Mia felt just like the waves crashing to the shore in the distance—turbulent and completely unable to slow the rising swell inside her. She whimpered as Max started to fuck her with his fingers, his strokes deep and hard, and he centered his total attention on the throbbing bud pleading for his attention. She drowned in sensation, rocking with the spasms that seized her body as she rode the most powerful climax she'd ever had. "Max. Oh, yes. Max." She ended up moaning and shouting, unable to help screaming his name as he eked every ounce of pleasure that he could wring from her body by slowly, sensually licking the cream from her orgasm.

Panting, not giving her a chance to recover, Max stood and stripped his sandy, soaked jeans from his body, taking his boxer briefs down with them. Picking up one of the condoms, he tore it open with his teeth and sheathed himself. After he finished, he was on her in a heartbeat, thrusting his powerful, naked body between her thighs. "I think you're the sexiest woman on earth," Max said, his voice rough and graveled. "Hearing you moan, scream my name, making you come. Fuck. There's no better feeling in the world. Except maybe having my cock inside you."

Barely over the effects of her climax, Mia needed this man all over again. The yearning was cell-deep and necessary, a desire that transcended mere lust. She needed to be taken by him, consumed by him, joined with him. Max was the other half of her soul, and she wanted him now. "Fuck me, Max. Please."

"Tell me you need me, Mia. 'Cause I know I fucking need you. I have to know you want me as much as I burn for you right now," he said, his voice tortured, before his mouth took hers, leaving her unable to speak the words that she needed to say.

Mia gave as good as she got, her tongue tangling with his as he kissed her senseless. Wrapping her arms around his shoulders, she could feel his powerful body shudder as he entered and retreated with his tongue again and again, as though he needed to master her, conquer her, make her his with his body. Her legs went around his waist, her heels resting against his rock hard ass, urging him to join them.

"I need you. I need you so much I can't stand it," Mia gasped as Max released her lips. "I love you, Max. Always have. Always will."

Truer words had never been spoken. She'd belonged to Max from the moment they'd met. She'd been running out of a coffee shop, her mind already on the multitude of tasks she'd needed to get done that day, when she'd run into Max. Literally. She'd dumped the contents of her large, non-fat latte down the front of his suit; she'd been mortified. He'd laughed, charming her immediately. And they were married six months later. Needing him, wanting him, had never been in question. Her insecurity was whether or not she was the right woman for him, the two of them being so very glaringly different, her past holding some ugly facts that she'd never revealed to him.

"And I love you, my beautiful, sexy Mia. Don't ever leave me alone again," he ordered arrogantly, though his velvety voice held a touch of vulnerability.

"I won't. I promise. Fuck me, Max. I can't wait any longer." One more moment without him inside her and she was going to lose it.

Max rolled, taking her with him, his powerful arms around her waist. His hands moved to her hips. "You fuck me, sweetheart. I want to see you. I want to watch you come this time."

She didn't hesitate. Grabbing his hard, throbbing cock, she impaled herself on him, moaning as he filled her almost to the point of pain. Almost…but not quite. Max was well endowed, and he stretched her to maximum capacity, the walls of her channel giving way and then capturing him inside her. Her hands were resting on his muscular chest, and she couldn't resist stroking his overheated skin, running her fingers over the light dusting of hair on his chest, smoothing over powerful biceps and shoulders. *God, he's a beautiful man.*

"Oh, hell yeah. Touch me. Make me believe you're really with me again," Max rasped, grasping her hips and pulling out of her, only to bring her down again. And again. "No. Fucking. Better. Feeling." Each word was punctuated with a thrust, a powerful slamming of his hips as he delivered each stroke.

Leaning forward, her body beginning to melt, Mia dropped her palms to the side of Max's head, moaning as he controlled the pace and intensity of his thrusts. She might be on top, but her husband was completely in control, and he hammered into her relentlessly, like a man possessed.

Mia could feel her impending climax, and her entire body quaked. "Max," she gasped, unable to verbalize anything else.

Removing his hands from her hips without slowing his pace, he grasped her hands in his, their fingers entwining as he captured her mouth. His tongue speared through her lips, mimicking the actions of his cock, and she bent to him, eager to be joined in every way she could be with this incredible man. Fingers entwined, their mouths fused together, and their bodies joined completely, Mia's heart beat as one with Max's. At that moment, they were exactly as they were supposed to be…completely woven and braided together, unsure of where one ended and the other began. She was teetering on the edge of orgasm, ready to plunge off the cliff to ecstasy. It was exhilarating. It was terrifying.

"Come for me, sweetheart. Let go," Max urged against her lips as he pulled his mouth from hers, his cock still thrusting deeper, harder, his groin grinding and stimulating her clit with every surge of his hips.

Her climax hit her like an avalanche—powerful, wild, and completely out of control. She rode the waves as they came, moaning with every strong pulsation. "It's too much. Too much."

Releasing her hands, Max held her hips, plunging into her again and again, frenzied as he found his own release. "Never enough. Never enough," he groaned, placing a hand on her ass to keep himself deeply inside her, as though he couldn't bear to be separated from her.

Mia collapsed on Max's chest, completely spent, and slightly disoriented, not quite sure how she had managed to live through the kind of passion she'd just experienced with her husband.

Neither one of them spoke, nor did they need to. Max's hand stayed possessively on her ass as his other splayed over her back, stroking lightly, soothingly. She absorbed the feeling of his hot breath on the side of her neck, the brush of his abrasive whiskers against her skin, and the steady, rapid beat of his heart beneath her fingertips.

Finally, her breathing and heart rate calm, she murmured, "Still hate this beach?"

"No. But now every time I come out here my cock will be hard," he grumbled, but his voice held a note of amusement.

Rubbing sensually against him, she answered, "Good. I'll come out with you."

"You damn well better," he insisted, slapping her playfully on the ass.

Leaning up, she rested her forehead against his. "You've certainly developed quite the potty mouth, Mr. Hamilton. I never knew you could talk that naughty."

"I'm not quite sure I can restrain it anymore," Max told her, sounding slightly disgruntled. "You've always made me crazy."

"Then don't hold back. I love you, Max. Nothing between us is wrong. You can talk dirty to me any time. It turns me on," she told him as she ran a palm down his whiskered cheek and jaw.

"Then I'll never try to control it." He took her hand from his face and brought it to his lips, kissing her palm reverently. "Don't come out here alone, Mia. I can't lose you again. I won't survive it."

His tone was deliciously bossy, but the tortured look on his face nearly killed her. Whatever she'd done, Max had suffered for it, and she hated herself for leaving, whatever the reason. She'd put him through hell, and she didn't even understand why. "I won't. I promise." There was a newness, an openness between them that she didn't want to see destroyed.

"See that you don't," Max said gruffly, disconnecting himself from her and disposing of the condom. He sat up, turned her position on his lap, and got to his feet with her still held tightly in his arms.

Mia fought to get Max to put her down, afraid he'd end up straining his back by carrying her up the stairs, but he just clutched her naked body tighter, his hold on her unyielding.

"I'll never let you go," he told her adamantly, more of a vow than a statement.

Mia gave in with a sigh. She couldn't argue about that. "The condoms. You didn't grab them. We might need them," she said a little shyly, thinking she was being a little presumptuous in thinking Max might want her again so soon.

Max's laughter boomed through the air as he entered the house. "Sweetheart, do you think I don't have some stashed in every nook and cranny of this house?" He gave her a lusty grin. "I did mention that it was a priority."

Relieved, she smiled back at him, her heart soaring at the fact that being with her had been so important to him, dire enough that he put condoms everywhere.

"Still feeling pretty ambitious?" she bantered, still not quite used to this new Max.

"Depraved and deprived," he told her, disgruntled.

"I think we can take care of that," she said longingly as Max carried her toward the bedroom.

"Oh, I'm planning on it," he answered in a cocky, haughty tone.

Mia sighed, speechless. She certainly wasn't going to argue about that.

Chapter 5

"**B**illionaire's Wife Returns From The Dead With No Memory!"

Mia flipped the newspaper over on the bed, her stomach sinking to her feet as she realized the media had caught up with her. "I hate the media," she commented vehemently, unable to keep the slight tremor from her voice.

Max came through the bedroom door with two cups of coffee in his hands, handing one to her before picking up the paper, glancing at it and dropping it into the trash can beside the bed. Seating himself on the bed next to her, splayed out like every women's fantasy in just a sexy pair of black silk boxer shorts, he replied, "Hey, don't let it upset you, sweetheart. I'll give a statement, they'll be hot on our trail for a while, and then they'll find something more interesting to write about. They always do."

Mia knew that, but while they were the hot topic, they'd hound them to death. Her eyes ran over Max lovingly, her pulse accelerating as she took in his powerful thighs, that tempting happy trail on his sculpted abs and his broad, naked chest. Finally, her gaze landed on his face, and the concern she saw there as he watched her closely over the rim of his coffee cup made her relax. "I'm sorry. I know it's part of our life, but they never let up after what happened with my parents..." Her voice trailed off, not really wanting to talk about her mother and father.

She'd grown up monetarily privileged, but all that proved was that even the wealthy could be incredibly dysfunctional. Her father had been a brilliant man in business, but he had been emotionally deranged, and everyone in her family had paid for it in one way or another, her mother with her life. She didn't want to be in the news, didn't want the murder/suicide of her parents to be dug up and talked about again. It had barely died down when she had met Max. Since then, she'd done everything possible to stay out of the media's gossip columns.

"They won't drag it up, Mia. I'll kill the first person who does," he said ominously.

Mia smiled, sipping her coffee and watching her husband, her heart skittering at his dangerous look. They should both be exhausted since they'd spent most of the night devouring each other, even after their passionate interlude on the beach. But strangely, she felt happier than she'd ever been, even though she was missing part of her past. And Max looked relaxed, even with the irritated expression he had on his gorgeous face from talking about the press.

"I don't care about me. I can handle it. I don't want them to talk about it because it would be hard on you, Kade, and Travis." She took another sip of her coffee, watching Max's expression turn from irritated to stunned.

"Me? Why the hell would I care?" Max drained his coffee cup and set it on the bedside table.

"I'm your wife. You're a billionaire businessman. I've always tried to be the woman you need—"

"You are the woman I need," he told her, his voice angry now. "I don't care who your parents were or what they did."

"My father was insane. He shot my mother and then put the gun in his mouth and blew his brains out. You think they won't wonder about my sanity? Whether I'm a little crazy too? I'm coming back from the dead, a big hole in my memory. I'm sure people will judge by my history." And God, she hated that.

"It's not your goddamn history," Max replied, the muscle in his jaw twitching as he answered. "And anyone who judges you by something your parents did isn't somebody we need to give a shit about. You, Kade, and Travis aren't made from the same mold."

"I've always tried to be careful, tried not to draw attention to myself. I wanted to be a good wife to you, Max. I tried to change. I don't know what happened." She understood what he was saying, but people did judge, they did talk, and Max had never been the subject of bad press. He was respected as a businessman, his personal life never dragged through the mud because he gave the media nothing to talk about.

"Did you feel like you needed to change because of me?" Max asked curiously, his voice calmer.

"Yes. No. I don't know. I wanted to be perfect. I slipped sometimes, did something stupid or thoughtless." Honestly, now that she thought about it, she'd turned herself inside out to become the woman she thought Max wanted. "Every time I got a lecture from you, I tried to laugh it off, but I tried to do better. But you were just so damned perfect," she replied honestly.

Max started with a snort, and then he rolled on the bed, his up-roarious laughter echoing off the walls of the enormous bedroom.

"What?" Mia drained her coffee cup and set it on the table.

Sitting up, Max took her by the shoulders, still chuckling as he told her adamantly, "Sweetheart, I'm far from perfect. Do you realize that I think we were both trying to fit the mold that we assumed was the other's ideal? It would be even more fucking hilarious if it wasn't a little heartbreaking." He eased her down on the pillows, and lay on his side, one arm draped around her waist and the other propping his head up, staring at her adoringly. "Tell me what you did."

Max seemed so approachable and amused that she decided to just tell him. They were starting again, so he might as well know exactly what she'd done to try to be the perfect wife. "I waxed. I hated it, but I screamed my way through it, cursing the woman doing it in my head as a sadist. And I tried to stop being so clumsy. I got up every day and primped, even though I just wanted to wear a tank top without a bra and a crappy pair of shorts and get to work. I dieted, trying to be slender, feeling like I was starving to death most of the time. I stopped cursing because I thought it offended you, although I came close to slipping occasionally. I was raised with two brothers, and watching what I said was difficult. And I bought clothes because they were trendy, not because I liked them. I bit my tongue at parties, even when I didn't agree with what people were saying." Nibbling at her lower lip, she watched his face as it broke into a sexy smile.

Max was silent for a moment before he replied. "One: I didn't like the waxing, but if you wanted it, I didn't care. Two: You're not clumsy—you're absolutely adorable. I think I fell in love with you the moment you spilled your coffee on my favorite suit, which never did recover. But I got you out of the deal, so I didn't give a shit about the suit. Three: All of your make-up was washed off when you jumped into the ocean last night, and your hair is wild like you've been well-satisfied. And you take my breath away. I'm all for the shorts and braless look, just know I might never leave the house after I see those incredible breasts. Four: You don't need to diet. Your figure was full and beautiful; you're active and healthy. Most of the time, I was fighting for control. Five: I want you to wear whatever you want and be exactly who you are. If some uptight prick at a party pisses you off, tell him off. Six: I couldn't care less if you curse. Especially if you want to talk dirty to me. But know that I'll take you exactly where you happen to be at that moment if you do that," he warned ominously. He brushed the hair from her face gently before adding, "I fell in love with you, Mia. I don't need you to be anyone other than who you are. I felt the distance growing after we were married, but I thought it was me. I was trying too hard to be the sensible man I assumed you wanted."

Mia had to admit, she was curious now. "What did you do? You told me about the trips to distance yourself. What else?"

"I did a lot of little things, like shaving twice a day, but leaving was the worst part. It nearly killed me to leave, but I always felt like I needed to get a grip because you wanted a steady husband instead of a maniacal beast who was obsessed with the woman he loved. To me, you've always been perfect, and I could never be good enough to deserve you. So instead, I ran away when I couldn't get my emotions under control," he said, his voice husky and dark. "I wasn't raised to show my emotions openly. And what I felt for you wasn't normal for me. I was terrified if you really knew how I felt...you'd run like hell. Most women would...or should."

"I wouldn't. I felt the same way, Max. I always have. But I guess I was convinced that you needed the perfect wife, and I was going to have to compromise or mold myself into that image to keep your love," Mia admitted, feeling once again like two different women in one body. "You were worldly, sophisticated, and completely controlled. I didn't want to smother you with emotion. And I felt... too much."

Max moved over her, his hot, muscular body hovering over hers, holding most of his weight from her body with his arms. "Suffocate me, Mia. Let me drown in your love and affection. Touch me. Shower me with your laughter. That's all I've ever wanted. I need that from you. I just want to be close to you." His face looked tortured but hopeful. "Please," he added hoarsely.

Mia closed her eyes, her heart pounding, completely destroyed by the look on Max's face. Her steady, calm, no-nonsense husband wanted to be loved. Really loved. He didn't want the perfect woman. He just wanted her, and all of the craziness that went along with a love so intense that neither one of them had been able to handle it. "I think I've grown up, Max. I'm not sure what happened to me, but I don't want to change anymore. If you think you can handle me, I'll give you all the love I have and leave you begging for a reprieve," she warned him playfully. "And I love you a whole hell of a lot. Can you handle that?"

His grin grew wicked as his gorgeous hazel eyes roved over her face. "Oh yeah."

Oh crap. I'll want to jump his bones every minute of every day if he keeps looking at me like this.

Their eyes met and held, and Mia lifted her hand to his rough jaw and caressed it softly as she pleaded, "Love me just like this forever. It's all I've ever wanted, too."

Max buried his face in her hair with a groan. "I will, sweetheart. I promise."

Mia sighed and wrapped her arms around him, stroking her hands over his back and to his waist, absorbing the heady, masculine scent and feel of the man she loved.

At that moment, everything was perfect.

The next morning, Mia watched Max from across the hospital waiting room with a smile. Kara had been in labor since three a.m., and every friend and family member of Simon's had shown up this morning in a show of support. Max and Helen Hudson, Sam and Simon's mother, were currently consoling Sam, trying to convince him that when Maddie had her baby, it wasn't going to be *that* bad. Maddie wasn't Kara's physician, but as a dear friend, Maddie had gone in to observe with the OB doctor. Nobody had seen Simon at all since he'd been unwilling to leave Kara's side, but Maddie came out with periodic progress reports.

"How damn long does it take to have a baby? She's been in labor forever," Sam grumbled loud enough that Mia could hear him across the small waiting room.

Maddie's last progress report about thirty minutes ago had been that Kara was getting ready to push. She'd also said that Simon swore he'd never touch Kara again. Maddie had delivered that comment with a snort, knowing Simon would forget that promise fairly quickly.

"It's her first baby, Sam. It takes time," Mia heard Helen tell her son patiently.

Looking to her right, Mia smiled weakly at Kade, not quite sure exactly why he was here, but glad that he was. She'd been able to give him the DNA results that had just come back from the lab.

"Do you hate me for having some doubts at first?" Kade asked quietly, his face solemn.

"You're my brother. I love you. I was presumed dead. So no, I don't hate you because you didn't immediately accept me," she replied honestly, although it *had* hurt a little. She'd always been close to her twin brothers, and she knew they had always protected her from the brunt of their father's crazy behavior. Kade was the brother who made her smile, and needing to prove herself to him had pained her, even though she logically understood why it had needed to be done.

"I was an asshole. I knew it was you from the moment you criticized my shirt and called me by name in the park, but all I could think about was what would happen if Max got attached and something happened. He was a mess, Squirt. He walked around like an empty shell, like he didn't care if he lived or died. Honestly, I don't think he *did* care. I didn't want to see him suffer anymore," Kade finished abruptly, as though he were uncomfortable talking about Max's grief. Or his own.

Mia clasped his hand gently and squeezed, glad her brother had been there for Max and that they'd grown close. She gave him a mock scowl as she answered, "I'm twenty-nine years old, almost thirty. Don't you think it's time to stop referring to me by that stupid childhood nickname?" God, she'd always hated it. When they were younger, she had prayed for a growth spurt that had never happened just so she could tower over Kade and Travis to make them stop teasing her about being vertically challenged. She was five foot four inches, not incredibly short, but her brothers were both nearly a foot taller than she was.

Kade grinned and winked at her. "Nope. You're still a squirt."

"And you still wear bad shirts," she reminded him fondly, looking at today's ensemble. She was guessing he'd toned it down for the hospital. Today he looked almost normal in a black t-shirt and jeans, emphasizing his attractive blond hair and blue eyes. No wonder the women had swooned over him in all fifty states when he was a pro football player. Women had been easily swayed, swearing their allegiance to his team just because Kade was playing. As his sister, she'd just rolled her eyes, laughing when every woman she knew wanted to meet him. Her brother had never been especially flirty, and he was far from a ladies' man. He'd been faithful to his longtime girlfriend for years, and the bitch had broken his heart.

Kade squeezed her hand back. "I just don't want you to think I'm not happy to have you back. I am. More than I can say. But I was worried about Max, too."

She looked up at him, meeting eyes so much like her own. "I'm glad. Really." Strangely, she was happy. If Kade had been trying to protect Max, it made her love her brother even more.

"He loves you, Mia. It just sucks that now I'll have to put up with all three of them acting like idiots over their women, one of them my sister." Kade nodded his head toward Sam and Max, and Mia knew he was including Simon in his statement, even though Simon was absent.

"You'll survive," she answered unsympathetically, knowing Kade just hadn't found the woman who was right for him. She'd never liked his ex-girlfriend, and although she didn't want to see her brother's heart broken, *she* definitely hadn't been *the one*.

Mia watched Max as he slapped Sam on the back and rose, strolling over to sit beside her.

"What are you two talking about?" Max asked casually, stretching his jean-clad legs out in front of him and eyeing both of them cautiously.

Mia flinched, knowing her reappearance had caused tension between her brother and her husband.

"Squirt refuses to feel sorry for me because I have to deal with you, Sam, and Simon freaking out about your females," Kade said woefully.

"You're still on my shit list, buddy," Max warned, glaring at Kade. "I'm offering a temporary truce because of the situation, but I still plan to pound you the first chance I get. If you said one word to upset her, I'll make you regret it."

"Yeah. Let's see you try it," Kade shot back, grinning. "I might have a lame leg, but I can still kick your ass."

"No mercy because of your leg. I'm not going easy because of it," Max warned him. "It's healed."

"I didn't expect you to. Give it your all. Just have an ambulance on standby when you decide to try it," Kade retorted amicably, as though he were talking about the weather instead of putting his buddy in the hospital.

Mia almost got whiplash looking back and forth between the two men—one apparently nonchalant, the other furious.

"Both of you stop," she ordered. "We're here for a happy occasion." She turned to her husband. "Kade was concerned about you. I don't blame him for that. I'm glad he was trying to protect you, because I love you." Turning to her brother, she poked her finger in his face. "And you behave. You're deliberately provoking him, and it's not amusing."

She faced forward, watching Sam and Helen talk but not able to hear their words clearly. She could feel two set of eyes on her, and finally, a large, muscular arm reached across her. *Kade's*.

"Kiss and make up, man." It was a smart ass comment, but Kade's tone was sullen.

"Fine. I'll kick your ass later," Max agreed, sticking his hand out to shake with Kade.

Mia bit her lip, wondering if the testosterone overload of sitting between the two men was going to kill her. "I'm glad you two can act like adults," she commented drily.

"Do I have a choice?" Max asked, settling back into his chair.

"Not if you want to get some later." Her sassy comment slipped out of her mouth before she could think better of it.

"Sweetheart, for *that*, I'd get down on my knees and beg."

Mia shivered, the reply low, sexy, and making the memories of the night before form in her mind with perfect recall.

"Shit. Give me a break. TMI. She's my damn sister." Kade's voice was disgusted as he rose from his chair. "I'm going for coffee. Anybody want anything?"

"Coffee," she and Max said in perfect synchrony.

They looked at each other and laughed. "Addict," Mia accused, still laughing.

"I caught the addiction from you," he accused, smiling now.

Truth was, they were both addicts and always had been. They had, after all, met outside a coffeehouse, both needing their fix that day.

Maddie came into the waiting room, her face shining with happiness. "She's beautiful. Eight pounds, one ounce, and completely healthy," she announced, hugging her husband as he rose to sweep her into a hug.

"Kara okay?" Sam asked, concerned.

"She's fine. Worn out, but good," Maddie replied. "If I can tear him away, I'll get Simon to bring the baby out of the delivery room so you can all see her."

Mia stood up, commenting happily, "I'm sure he's a proud daddy."

"He will be. He's a little green around the gills at the moment. I didn't think he was going to make it through the delivery. Kara was calmer than he was," Maddie said jovially, planting a kiss on her husband's cheek.

Everyone was on their feet, all talking at once, marveling over the birth of Helen's first grandchild and Sam's new niece.

Max grasped her hand tightly, keeping her at his side protectively. Slapping Sam on the back, he told his friend jokingly, "Your turn next, buddy."

Sam's smile faded and his usually tan complexion turned white as he looked down at his wife. "I don't think I can do it," he told Maddie, his voice full of dread.

"You don't have to do it. I'm doing it," Maddie answered calmly. "Since everybody is here, I guess we can tell you all. Sam and I are being twice blessed. We're having twins."

"Oh shit," Mia heard Max mumble under his breath, but he was so close only she could hear him. She squeezed his hand, warning him not to make his concern show. It was obvious that Sam was already sick with worry.

Sam sat down, his face white, looking like he needed to put his head between his legs to keep from passing out. No wonder he had been fretting so much over childbirth.

Mia smiled at Maddie, whose happiness was showing in her eyes. Obviously her sister-in-law was overjoyed, and it made Mia's heart warm. Wrapping her arms around Maddie, Mia whispered, "Congratulations, Maddie. We'll help the guys get through it," she said jokingly, although she wasn't so sure the statement wasn't true.

"I just told Sam," Maddie admitted, hugging Mia back. "He'll warm to the idea eventually."

Both women looked at Sam, his face white as a sheet now.

"Or not," they both said together, laughing as Helen joined in the group female hug, leaving the men to ponder the hell of having twins.

She and Max waited until they could see the baby before they left, walking hand in hand out of the front entrance of the hospital after viewing Simon's adorable baby girl, completely surrounded by Max's security to keep the media away.

"I wish I could have your baby," she pondered thoughtfully.

"Sweetheart, you don't say something like that to me and not expect me to respond accordingly. I thought you wanted to wait," Max said huskily.

Mia thought for a minute before answering, knowing she was ready to have Max's child. In fact, she was starting to ache to have his baby. "I know we were waiting to have a family, but—"

"I'm ready if you are. I think we've waited long enough to start really living our lives together," he told her warmly, wrapping an arm around her waist.

"Me, too," she replied, surprising herself with that answer. She hadn't been ready before, but suddenly she couldn't wait to have Max's child, to see a child created with love grow inside her. Maybe she really had grown up.

Two women in the same body…again.

For some reason, she liked the woman she was now. "When I recover my memory, we can talk about it," she replied. "We do need some time after all that's happened, but it would be nice to plan it."

The Billionaire's Salvation

"I'll be more than happy to do my part to help," Max replied, his voice intense and sensual, as though he couldn't wait to get her naked.

"You'll be my stud once I know what happened and we know everything is going to be okay?" she asked teasingly.

"Baby, I *am* your stud. The only one you'll ever need. And everything will be fine," he quipped arrogantly.

"We can't exactly get started immediately, but you could practice," she dared him, heat gathering between her thighs and branching outward.

They'd used his car and driver, and he helped her into the back seat of the limo, closing the privacy barrier as he climbed in after her.

Grinning wickedly at her, he hit a button that opened a slanted storage compartment, causing condoms to pour out and onto the floor.

"You have condoms in the car? You really are prepared," she said, laughing as he tore open a random package.

"I was a Boy Scout," he informed her in a sinful voice.

Naughty Max was overwhelmingly seductive, and she had no defense against him. Not that she wanted any. She was more than willing to let him practice, and he did.

Chapter 6

*I*t was sixty-five degrees, but Mia was sweating. The beads of moisture were trickling down her face, one right after the other, her body trembling as she did as she was ordered and looked down the scope of the rifle, only to jerk her head back when she saw her husband's head right in the center of the sight, vulnerable. "No! Don't hurt him. I'll do whatever you want. Just leave my family alone," she cried desperately, yanking against the steely grip restraining her.

The rifle slowly lowered, the maniacal voice holding her hostage declaring, "Easy shot. A few hundred yards. I could take him out in less than ten seconds and then go pick off both your brothers, too, before anybody even realizes what happened. The security of these rich pukes isn't worth a shit."

He could. Mia knew he could. Danny Harvey had always been a sharpshooter, highly skilled at hitting his target. "You won't get away with it. The police—"

"Won't do you a damn bit of good after they're dead. And I doubt they'll pay much attention before that. Everyone knows about the crazy Harrisons. They'll never find me," he answered venomously.

"Are you willing to take that chance?" In a softer, crazy sing-song voice, he told her, "You don't love any of them, Mia. Not like you love me. You want me. You married that rich suit as a substitute. I'm here now. Cooperate and we can be together again."

She cringed as his large, grimy hand touched her cheek. "What do you want, Danny?"

"You. We belong together. We always have," he told her harshly.

"And my money," she added in a self-mocking voice. Danny would have no problem working his way through her trust fund now that she had access to it.

Grabbing a fistful of her hair, he slammed her head back against the tree he had been propped up against just a moment ago. "That's just a side benefit. I love you."

This isn't love. It had never been love. It was insanity.

The blow to her skull making her dizzy, Mia shook her head, trying to clear her mind. Danny was right about one thing…she couldn't risk it. And she wouldn't. She had to figure out a way to get Danny away from her family before they all ended up dead like her parents. He was more toxic than her father had been, and even more deadly.

It's my fault. I brought this bastard into my life, and now he's threatening everyone I care about. I should have never married Max. I should have stayed away from him. He doesn't deserve this.

A set of cold, slimy lips clamped down against hers, and Mia tried to choke down the bile rising in her throat, willing herself not to struggle. It would be a fight against a madman, and she'd lose. She needed to think. If she didn't, Max and her brothers could die.

Focusing on thoughts of Max, she tried to block out everything except her husband until Danny had finally stopped grinding his mouth on hers, leaving her lip bleeding.

"I can think of a better use for that mouth," he said in his lunatic voice. He pushed her to her knees and ripped open the fly of his jeans, his member flopping out in front of her face. "Suck me. You know you want to."

Tears flowed down her cheek as she eyed the flesh in front of her face, starting to gag from the noxious odor of an unwashed body and filthy clothing.

I can't do this. I can't do this.

But one thought of Max, the thought that he was about to board a plane taking him out of harm's way, and she did the unthinkable, complying with what the psychopath wanted, blocking out everything except getting through the degrading act, giving Max enough time to be airborne.

She heard the revving of the airplane's engine, giving her hope as she finally gagged, trying to pull away from the body in front of her, but she couldn't move, the grip on her to hold her head in place relentless.

She gagged just as the plane moved down the runway.

And then she vomited, and for that involuntary reaction, she was severely punished.

Mia woke gasping for air, sitting straight up in bed, her hand to her stomach to fight her nausea, her body moist and the sheets wet with her sweat.

It was a nightmare. Just a horrible dream.

Still, she was panting as she slid her feet to the floor and stumbled to the master bathroom, completely naked. She closed the door and flipped on the light, staring at the terrified face looking back at her in the mirror. It was her, a person she recognized, no longer two women in the same body, but one woman who had changed in the last few years. Suddenly, she knew who she was, and all of the memories that had eluded her came flooding back in a rush of knowledge that overwhelmed her senses.

Shivering, she flipped on the shower, letting the water get hot before stepping inside, hoping the warmth would take away the cold chill running up her spine from the shock of recovering her memory. Fear spiked her adrenaline, making her entire body ready for flight.

Run. Run. Run. I can't stay here. I have to leave. I have to protect Max.

Mia poured body wash into her hand, using it liberally, trying to scrub away the memories of her dream. Pain tore through her chest at the knowledge that she couldn't stay with Max. Not if she really loved him. And she did. So much that it was tearing her apart.

Almost as if she'd willed it, Max was suddenly behind her, his arm coming possessively around her waist, his solid, muscular body supporting her.

"Miss me?" he asked in a husky voice against her ear. "You should have woken me up and taken me with you."

Oh God, she'd like to take him with her wherever she went, never having to be away from him again. Max was the other half of her soul, and the thought of being separated from him ever again nearly killed her. She turned and wound her arms around his neck, resting her head against his shoulder as she held him, skin to skin, against her. She wanted to memorize the feel of him, try to absorb his essence into her soul. "Bad dream. I was all sweaty," she murmured, hoping he wouldn't ask too many questions. Not now.

"Then you definitely should have woken me up. I love being all sweaty with you." Taking her lightly by the shoulders, he pulled her back to look into her eyes, tipping her chin up with his strong fingers. "Hey. Are you okay?"

"Yeah. I'm good now," she lied hastily, wanting to cry as she saw the concern in his beautiful eyes.

I need one more memory. Something good to replace the bad.

Her fingers still slick with soap, she ran her hand slowly down his body, tracing every hard muscle of his chest, moving slowly down the sexy trail of hair that led to his groin. Without hesitation, she grasped his cock and stifled a moan, finding him already hard and ready. She wanted him inside her, but even more than that, she wanted to exorcise old ghosts, and she knew exactly how to do it.

Cupping the back of his head, she urged his lips to hers, desperate to feel his mouth locked with hers, his tongue thrusting, warming her as nothing else could. He responded immediately, his hands coming up to her head to hold it in place as he groaned into her mouth as he took it, his need already red hot from having her slippery fingers run over and over his engorged member, teasing but not really satisfying him. She opened to him, letting him plunder her mouth, master her senses. It was a kiss of desperation and need, and she gave in to it, savoring Max's possession.

Finally, he moved his mouth from hers, leaving her nearly breathless. She slid down his body until she was on her knees, in the same position that she had been in her nightmare. But this...this was real. And this was Max. And there was nothing she wanted more than to pleasure him. She let the water wash away the soap as she cupped his ass with both hands and replaced her teasing fingers with her mouth, letting every thought slip away except the man she loved.

Max nearly came the moment Mia took him into her mouth, her blatant sexuality almost making him come undone. *Jesus H. Christ!* The feel of that velvety tongue on his cock, the friction of her enthusiastic sucking was enough to make him lose his mind. She was the sexiest woman he'd ever known, and she was becoming completely sexually uninhibited, which was driving him to the brink of insanity.

My wife. All mine.

He slapped one hand against the tiled wall of the enclosure to keep himself steady, the hot water hitting him in the chest as Mia attacked his cock with more enthusiasm than skill. But it didn't matter. Every touch was exquisite, every movement erotic. "Mia. I won't last." Nope. He wouldn't. He wasn't going to make it through the next minute without having a heart attack.

He speared his hand into her wet hair, gently guiding her head, and released a strangled groan that he couldn't stop from escaping his lips. Looking down, he watched her take him between those gorgeous lips again and again, and the visual of the woman he loved pleasuring him made his balls tighten almost unbearably.

Fuck. Fuck. Fuck.

Fire was licking through his groin. He was torn between urging her harder, faster—or hauling her up and thrusting himself inside her warm, welcoming heat. He had condoms in the bathroom drawer; he could…

Mia moaned, and Max watched, completely mesmerized, as she slid one hand up the inside of her thigh and slipped her fingers between her folds, touching herself with no other intent except to make herself come with him. It was the hottest damn thing Max had ever seen. Her fingers worked between her thighs as she brought her other hand up to work with her mouth to send him completely over the edge.

"Come with me, Mia," he demanded, gritting his teeth and throwing his head back as she moaned continually against his flesh, vibrating his cock until his head nearly blew off his shoulders. "Come with me."

His orgasm was wild and volatile, his whole body shuddering as he groaned his release, Mia never taking her mouth from him as she trembled from her own climax.

Max scooped her up and pulled her pliant body against him, wrapping his arms around her, knowing he held his whole world in his arms.

He rinsed them both gently and shut off the water. After drying them both, he carried his wife back to bed and held her, wondering how he had been lucky enough to get another chance with the one woman who rocked his entire universe.

They fell asleep entwined together, two pieces fit together perfectly. Max fell asleep in a world of total happiness and contentment.

When he woke up in the morning, Mia was gone.

It didn't take Max long to panic. He hadn't been concerned when he'd woken up to find his wife was already out of bed. The worry had started to set in when he couldn't find her anywhere in the house.

"Shit," he mumbled under his breath as he opened the door that led to the beach. "Mia," he bellowed, getting no reply. There was no sign she had gone outside. The back door had been locked, something she wouldn't do if she had ventured out to the beach.

Grabbing his cell phone, he checked with his security team, but she wasn't with them, and nobody had seen her leave the house.

Disconnecting, he hit another number, waiting impatiently as it rang.

"This better be important. It's early," Kade's rough, graveled voice answered.

"Mia's missing," Max told him irritably. "Is she there?"

"Hell no, she's not here. I was sleeping. What happened?" Kade answered, sounding more alert.

Max released a disappointed breath before he answered, "Nothing happened. She's just not here. Nobody saw her leave. Neither of the cars is missing." He froze as he entered the dining room and saw Mia's phone, keys, and a piece of paper lying on the dining room table.

"Hold on. I found something," Max told Kade, cradling the phone between his shoulder and ear as he moved the keys and snatched up the paper. His eyes scanned the words quickly.

> *Max,*
>
> *My memory finally returned and I remember everything. I left you voluntarily. I didn't think our relationship was going well and I thought it was time to separate.*
>
> *I'll have divorce papers served as soon as I can.*
>
> *Mia*

"What the fuck?" Max cursed violently into the phone, grabbing it as he tossed the note onto the table.

"What? What happened?" Kade asked anxiously, totally awake now.

"She's left me. On purpose. She doesn't want to be married anymore," Max told him robotically, unable to comprehend the words Mia had written as he told Kade what was in the brief and impersonal note.

"Bullshit," Kade's voice exploded through the phone. "She's in love with you. You know she is."

"I can't make her stay if she doesn't want to," Max answered, feeling like his heart was shattering. "She never wanted to be with me. She just didn't remember."

"You never gave up on her, man. Not once. Don't give up now. There's something going on that we don't know about," Kade argued, sounding like he was getting dressed as he was speaking, his voice muffled.

"Nobody forced her to write that note. Nobody is forcing her to leave. She made her fucking choice. Twice. Obviously she remembered that she didn't love me," Max uttered quietly, resigned. He'd spent years believing, never giving up, only to have her leave him once he'd found her again. To hell with her. He couldn't do this anymore. He'd been deluding himself all along, thinking that Mia loved him the same way he loved her. She obviously…didn't.

"Max, you know her. You know this isn't Mia. We need to figure out what's going on," Kade said urgently.

Max plopped onto the couch, everything he'd always believed completely shattered. At that point, he didn't know what to believe. All he knew was that he was imploding, and his whole world was being torn apart. "Truth is, maybe I never really knew her at all," he replied brokenly.

He disconnected the call and stared blankly at the opposite wall, trying to bury his emotions, trying to force them deep inside until he was completely numb. He knew if he didn't, he'd never survive.

Chapter 7

Kade Harrison entered his brother Travis' office at Harrison Corporation without knocking, shoving against the solid oak hard enough to make the door swing with powerful force and slam against the wall with a massive *thud*. Ignoring the sound, Kade focused on his brother, sitting behind his desk, buried in a mass of paperwork. Travis looked at Kade briefly, and then his eyes returned to his work, apparently unconcerned that Kade had nearly broken the heavy wood door.

Kade wasn't surprised to find his brother in his office, even though it was Saturday. Travis was always in the office. He was pretty sure his brother had a secret apartment hidden away in this building where he slept a few hours before returning to his office again.

Dropping into the chair in front of his brother's desk, he simply asked, "Where is she?"

Travis looked up again, his gaze narrowing as he met Kade's scowl. "Who?"

"Mia," Kade hissed impatiently, watching his brother's face. They were fraternal twins, Travis older than him by a mere twenty minutes, but they shared the same blue eyes. But while Kade was fair like his mother and Mia, Travis' hair was as black as a raven's wing, his features resembling those of their father. "She couldn't have done this alone. And there's only one person I know who could pull this off." Dammit, he knew Travis knew something. Mia was an intelligent woman, but she had to have had an accomplice, someone close to her to help her disappear so thoroughly for over two years. No one could cover their own tracks that well. And nobody was as painstakingly detailed and as cunning as his twin. This deed had Travis written all over it. "Two disappearances with no sign of her? Where is she, Travis? This is killing Max."

Travis sat back in his chair, lacing his fingers together behind his head. "What do you mean...two? She's back."

"She's gone again," Kade stated flatly, eyeing his brother's expression for a moment, fairly certain Travis didn't know she had fled...this time. The two of them disagreed on almost everything, but they were twins, and they could still read each other well. *Sometimes too well.*

"Shit. I brought her back. Did she recover her memory?" Travis asked urgently, sitting up and placing his hands on his desk.

"Yeah. What difference does that make?" Kade asked warily.

"It makes all the difference. I have something I needed to tell her as soon as her memory returned. I needed to tell her not to run. She doesn't have to anymore," Travis said angrily, although Kade could see it for exactly what it was...fear.

Kade's jaw clenched as he rasped, "You helped her disappear the first time?"

"Yes."

"And you didn't tell me she wasn't dead?" Kade wanted to get up and pound his brother to within an inch of his life. Travis, his own damn twin, had let him think his sister was dead. "Why?"

"She was in trouble. Her life was in danger and so were yours and Max's. If keeping my mouth shut to keep everyone alive was what I had to do...I did it." Travis' fist crashed down on the desk, making every item on the surface tremble and roll. "Do you think it was easy for me not to say anything, to watch everyone grieve? Contrary to what you might think, brother...I don't enjoy seeing you or Max suffer."

"You weren't close to Max; you didn't see how much he—"

"Because I couldn't," Travis answered angrily.

Travis could be a coldhearted bastard when he wanted to be, but Kade knew he loved his family. Although he was still pissed, Kade had to know what happened. "Tell me everything. And start at the beginning."

"We don't have time for that right now. I'll tell you everything later. We need to find Mia. She has to be scared. She doesn't know the man who was threatening everyone's life is no longer a problem." Travis stood and reached for his suit jacket, pulling it on in jerky motions, acting nothing like his usual calm, controlled self.

"And why is that?" Kade replied, rising to stand beside his brother.

"He's dead," Travis remarked with deadly calm. "Unfortunate accident."

"You should have shared this with me. You're my goddamn brother," Kade told him, his tone hostile. That Travis had kept this knowledge to himself for so long still made Kade want to throttle him. Travis always thought he knew what was best for everyone, spent more time trying to fix everyone and everything else except himself.

Travis turned to him abruptly, piercing him with a cold stare. "Why? What would you have done? Gone to find her, thinking we could protect her? Told Max so he could go find her?"

"Probably. She didn't need to do this. We have security—"

"Agents who failed to protect her from a madman," Travis informed his brother bitterly. "Max was gone, you were gone...and I was left to make a decision. So I made it. So go ahead...beat the shit out of me for trying to protect our little sister, for never wanting to see her debased and abused again. Had you or Max gone after her, she would have never stayed hidden, never been safe. I'll live with your hatred if it means you're all alive," Travis finished with the ruthlessness of a man who had always done whatever he had to do, his blue eyes glacial and dangerous as he eyed his twin.

Kade flinched, hating it when Travis drilled him with that eerie, arctic glare. "I suppose I need to hear you out. I want to know what happened. You'll tell me about it on our way to find Mia," Kade grumbled, knowing he wasn't going to like what his brother had to say. Much as Travis could be a pain in the ass, he was the glue that kept their family together, the problem solver, the doer of dirty jobs that had to be done.

Travis nodded once curtly and walked toward the door. "I'm pretty sure I know where she is. We'll have awhile to talk." Travis stopped at the door, his eyes traveling down Kade's chest and torso as he mentioned casually, "That's probably the most butt-ugly shirt I've ever seen on you. Congratulations on topping the puke green one with the ugly frogs."

Kade grinned. "I knew you'd like it." He followed Travis out the door and to the elevator.

"Are you ever going to grow up?" Travis asked blandly as he stepped into the elevator.

"Not if I can help it." Kade's grin grew broader as he watched his twin's disgruntled expression.

"You're changing your shirt, right? I'm not traveling with you if you're wearing that shirt."

"Sure. I can change. We just have to stop by my house after we tell Max," Kade answered with a deadpan expression. "I can pick up some extra clothes if we're going to be gone overnight to go get Mia."

Travis looked relieved. "Good."

Kade had no problem with changing his attire. He had a whole closet full of similar shirts at home that he could change into. Despite the urgency of the situation, he snickered quietly as the elevator doors closed.

Later that day, Mia arrived at her grandmother's forty-acre ranch in Montana, exhausted and deflated, her heart completely shattered. Two weeks ago, she'd gone to Tampa because Travis had sent a team of security to get her, telling her he needed her to come back to Florida. She hadn't even had a chance to find out why he had contacted her and wanted her to come back. She hadn't had any contact with Travis, or anyone else from Florida for that matter, since she'd fled the state, bound for Montana, over two years ago. Not until recently, when she'd finally seen them again, not knowing that she hadn't laid eyes on any of their beloved faces for over two years.

Coming back to Montana this time had been so much different from the time she'd come here to hide, to disappear. No one had been here for years before she had come back to the ranch over two years ago, and even Travis had needed to be reminded that she did have a home here.

She hadn't been sent on Travis' private jet in secrecy *this* time. She'd flown commercial under her own name, leaving a trail so obvious that anyone could find her. It had been done intentionally, to draw attention to the fact that she'd left Tampa. The media had uncovered the fact that she wasn't dead, and she'd need to lead evil away from the people she loved. If that led malevolence in her direction, it was all for the best. It was better that Danny Harvey find *her* rather than someone she loved. Let him come after her. She no longer cared. If he knew that she wasn't dead, he *would* find her, but it was better to be as far away as possible from her family. She'd be the bait, the lure that brought Danny here, far from Max and her brothers.

Even if Danny doesn't kill me, even if he does something and goes back to jail...I'll never be able to go back to Max. I'll never put him in harm's way again for something stupid I did in my past.

Mia exited her compact rental car, using the moonlight to find her way up the steps of the ranch style house, the place that she had called home for the last two and a half years. Digging in the dirt of the wilting potted plant next to the door, she grasped the key to the house, dusted her hands on her jeans and opened the door. She flipped on the lights, getting welcome relief from the darkness, thinking it was too bad that it couldn't illuminate the dimness of her heart and soul. The house still looked the same: comfortable leather furniture in the living room, the stone fireplace that brought coziness on cold Montana winter nights, and tons of memories of the grandmother who had taught her to make her first piece of jewelry right here in this home. She'd found peace here; she'd found herself here. But now, she could feel nothing except a hopelessness that nearly swallowed her whole. There had never been a time when she hadn't yearned for Max, but after seeing him again, the pain of separation was unbearable.

Dropping her purse and house key onto the couch, she made her way to the kitchen, glancing at the clock to make sure it wasn't too late to call Maude and Harold, her closest neighbors. The ranch was small by Montana standards, a hobby ranch, but it still left her isolated. Maude and Harold watched the ranch when no one was here, which had been all of the time for many years before she had moved in over two years ago. She dialed their number, explaining that she was back and they didn't need to come over daily anymore to care for the horses. It was something she actually enjoyed doing, and the reason her hands were rough and not manicured. And the exercise around the ranch had slimmed her body naturally. After a short chat with Maude, she hung up, exhausted just from trying to sound cheerful on the phone. Everything was an effort, and trying to pretend like everything was okay was painful. It wasn't okay. Max was completely gone from her life, and it felt like she had lost part of herself, a portion that she'd never find again.

You're Mia Hamilton. You don't have to be Mary Peterson anymore.

She had been Mary Peterson to everyone except Maude and Harold, who knew exactly who she was from her visits when she was younger, when she had spent her summers here with her grandmother. They had been friends with her gran, and there was no way she could have fooled them. Even though it had been years, they remembered her, but they had kept her secret. There had been very few others who really knew her—even as Mary Peterson. She'd lived in isolation at this ranch, making trips to Billings only for supplies, to sell her jewelry, and for her counseling sessions.

It doesn't matter if everyone knows who I am now. It's not like I'm keeping any secrets anymore. I'm trying to lure Danny here, away from my family.

Still, it was unlikely that anyone would recognize her, even though she wasn't planning to hide her real identity anymore. Her neighbors were too busy on their ranches to read social gossip from Florida, and she had always stayed out of the media as much as possible. Even when she went to Billings to see acquaintances again, no one would know who she was, who her parents had been, if she told them her real name. That was one thing she loved about living here. People here either liked her or they didn't because of the person she was, not because of how much money she had or who her family was.

Mia walked back through the living room, down the hallway and into one of the bedrooms that she had converted into a workshop. As usual, the room was chaotic, exactly as she had left it. But the disorder was an organized mess. She knew where every stone, decorative bead, and piece of metal was located. In the absence of availability of the gems and metals she had usually worked with, Mia had started working on Native American inspired pieces of jewelry and had found her niche as she never had in working on fancy jewelry without any real meaning to her. Now, every piece she made was a labor of love, every article containing a part of her as she'd crafted each ring, bracelet, and pair of earrings.

Miraculously, her unique items had caught on, and she sold enough to make a living, never really needing to touch the money Travis sent.

That's why I watch prices; I don't overspend. I wanted to make my own way, and I did. The only time she had used the money Travis had sent was to buy her rather old pickup truck, a necessity when one lived so far from town.

Wandering aimlessly, she walked into her bedroom, her eyes darting to her dresser immediately.

It's still here.

Without really thinking about her actions, she went to the dresser, picked up her wedding ring and slipped it on her finger. Wearing it brought in equal parts happiness and sorrow.

I should have never seen him again. I should have waited to talk to Travis and left.

"Now he'll really hate me," she whispered to herself, her voice filled with anguish. But she'd needed to do it, needed him to hate her and never try to seek her out.

God, she'd missed him so much. There hadn't been a day since she'd left him the first time that she hadn't ached to see him, hadn't felt like part of her was missing. While she'd had the hole in her memory, she couldn't remember what it had felt like to be away from him. Now, she remembered, and it had hurt like hell. Her only solace had been that her family was safe.

She tried to take the ring off again, but she couldn't do it. The weight of the platinum band and beautiful diamonds gave her a small measure of comfort. It wasn't much, but it was something.

Walking back to the kitchen, she dialed Travis' office number, but he didn't answer. He'd apparently changed cell phone numbers during the last few years, and she didn't know his current number. Trying Kade's number, she got his voicemail, hanging up without leaving a message. Kade rarely carried his cell phone, a habit he had acquired from being in the public limelight for so long, his phone ringing constantly and leaving him with no peace unless he turned it off and left it at home.

Her hand hovered over the numbers on the phone, so damn tempted to call Max just to tell him how sorry she was, how much she loved him.

"No!" she told herself harshly, putting the phone back in its cradle. "You can't talk to him ever again. You need to separate yourself from him completely. You're dangerous to him."

There was so much Max didn't know, so much she'd never told him. What would he think of her if he really knew how stupid she'd been, how very damaged she'd become from her past?

Two women in one body.

Now she knew exactly why she'd felt that way. She'd only remembered the woman she had been before she'd gone to counseling, before she'd found out how to deal with her past, and had actually begun to like the woman she had found underneath all of her dysfunctional self.

Max had fallen in love with an illusion, a woman who she'd tied in knots to please him, creating a persona that wasn't real. Max didn't truly know her at all. He never had.

I never really knew Max completely either, yet I loved him. I still do.

Mia slammed her thoughts closed, not wanting to think about the agony of still loving Max the way she did. He hadn't revealed all about his emotions, but he wasn't hiding the kind of secrets that she had never told him about, the horrible parts of her past. What would he think of a woman who had been stupid enough to be involved with a man who had no conscience, no qualms about killing anyone she cared about? Her father had been insane. Danny was a murderous sociopath.

Mia could hear the car coming up the drive before it arrived at the house, tires crunching over dirt and gravel as a vehicle made its way down her long, winding driveway. Her heart started to hammer and she ran to the kitchen to snatch the cordless phone, her hand trembling as she grabbed for it. Even though she was willing to sacrifice anything to keep Max and her brothers safe—and she intended to do just that—she didn't look forward to the actual consequences of her actions. She could be dead long before the police arrived.

Peering through the window right next to the front door and switching on the porch light, she watched a sleek black sports car pull up next to her rented vehicle. A shadowy figure emerged—a very large, very tall figure. Unable to make out his face, she squinted to bring his features into focus as he entered the circle of light cast by the porch lamp.

He stumbled, taking an uneven step as he cursed and moved forward again, his entire body finally revealed. Mia's legs practically gave out with relief, and then horror.

Max. Oh my God. No!

He finally made his way ungracefully to the door and disappeared from view. Mia could still hear him mumbling as he pounded on the wood, calling out, "Open the door, Mia. I know you're there."

Scrambling to the door, she unlocked it and swung it open.

For the first time in his life, Max looked truly bedraggled.

For the first time in his life, Max looked completely drunk and disorderly.

And, for the first time in his life, Max did *not* look happy to see her.

Chapter 8

It was a sad, sad situation when a man needed a healthy amount of Dutch courage just to face his own wife!

Max was drunk, and he knew it. Okay…he sort of knew it, but was trying like hell to convince himself that he wasn't. Maybe sitting at the end of Mia's driveway and taking some shots from the bottle of rotgut whiskey he'd bought in Billings hadn't been such a good idea. At the moment, he was alternating between being "king of the world" and "emperor of the dumbasses."

"Max…have you been drinking?" Mia asked, astonished.

Bingo. Give the woman a prize.

"I've had a few," Max answered, lying his ass off. He'd had more than a few. Several? A lot? Yeah…he thought one of those would be more accurate.

Still, seeing her in front of him, looking as beautiful as she always did, dressed casually in a pair of jeans and a red tank top, nearly killed him. Maybe the alcohol hadn't helped ease the pain at all, 'cause his chest was aching just from looking at her. She looked…concerned and anxious, and when he saw her blue eyes flash with fear, he nearly lost it. Was she afraid of him, or the whole confrontation thing? She did seem to prefer to run away. But then, he'd done it, too. He just hadn't done it with another woman.

"You never drink much," she mumbled, standing back to let him in. "And you never drink and drive."

Nope. He usually didn't. In fact, he'd never actually been drunk, which may be the reason he was having such a hard time deciding whether or not he truly *was* intoxicated. "Didn't drive while I was drinking—except up your driveway, which, by the way, has a hell of a lot of damn potholes." And in his possibly inebriated state, he'd driven into every one of them.

He was sauntering into the living room, trying hard not to fall on his ass, when he heard a stifled laugh.

"You're completely plastered, Max," Mia informed him, her eyes concerned, but her lips smiling slightly. "How much did you drink?"

"Don't know," he answered honestly. 'Cause really, he didn't remember how many swigs he'd taken from the bottle. He'd wanted enough to make him numb, enough to keep him from reacting to Mia. The thing was, he didn't think there was enough alcohol in the world to accomplish *that*.

"How did you know I was here?" she questioned carefully.

"Your brothers. I'm not sure…but I think I killed Travis," he answered cheerfully. He was pretty sure Travis wasn't dead, but he'd be battered and bruised, and the idea of *that* made Max pretty damn happy.

"You didn't kill my brother, and you shouldn't have gotten in a fight with him. He's just trying to protect me," she told him calmly, her hands on her hips as she looked up at him. "Is that how you got that cut over your eye? It's bleeding."

Damn. Travis *had* gotten a few punches in while trying to protect himself. But at the moment, Max was feeling no pain. "Yeah? If you think I look bad, you should see *him*," Max grumbled, highly offended that Mia hadn't taken him seriously when he'd said he had killed her brother. "He fights like a girl," he added, knowing he was lying. Had Travis really tried, and had Kade not stopped the fight,

Max had no doubt both of them would be in the emergency room right now. "Bastard should have told me. You're my goddamn wife. I had a right to know that you'd left me for another man."

Mia reached out and lightly touched the bruises on his face. "Oh, Max. What did they say? That isn't—"

"I want to hate you. I should hate you. But dammit, I just fucking can't," Max said coarsely, hating himself for still not being able to look at her and conjure up the hatred he should have for a wife who had left him desolate and heartbroken for over two years, making everything he'd felt—and still felt—seem like one big joke...at his expense. "Did you know that when I thought you were dead, I wanted to die too? I didn't want to go on living without you." Max knew they were drunken words, a pity party for one, but he didn't give a shit. "I was completely obsessed with you, so out of control that I had to back away from it to keep a leash on myself. And the whole fucking time, your mind was on another man." He reached out and grasped her wrist, pulling her down with him to the leather sofa, her body beneath his. He might be drunk, but as he looked down at her, he couldn't mistake the anguished, tormented look in her eyes. Did she feel sorry for him? *Christ.* He hoped not. The last thing he wanted was her pity.

"I'm not sure what my brothers said, but—"

"They told me you left me because of another man. They told me that you'd been hiding out in Montana at your grandmother's ranch. All this fucking time, you've been alive and content in another state, happily living your life while I tormented myself with thoughts that you were dead, that I'd never fucking see you again," Max growled, angry now that he'd gotten over feeling sorry for himself. He'd never been soul mates with this woman. Everything between them had always been a lie. "Why marry me? It wasn't like you didn't have your own money," he rasped, pissed that he had ever been such a sucker for her beautiful eyes and sweet demeanor. "And where the hell is this other guy? Did you run away from him, too?"

She struggled beneath him, twisting and turning to free her arms from the bulk of his body on top of hers. "I married you because I loved you. I didn't want anyone else." Finally her arms came free and she grabbed him on both sides of his head, staring fiercely into his eyes.

Max stared back, losing himself in the depths of a pair of shimmering blue eyes that had never failed to mesmerize him. Always had. And at that moment, just for a brief period of time, he wanted so damn badly to believe her. Because right now…nothing made sense. His mind was whirling from an overabundance of alcohol and all he could see was Mia's fiery eyes and tempting lips, and kissing her seemed like something he had to do, he needed to do, and to hell with everything else. Grasping her wrists, he pinned them over her head and almost groaned as her breasts jutted out and brushed his chest. He swooped down and covered her mouth with his, sipping from her like a man dying of thirst. She opened to him immediately, like a flower that had just been waiting to fully bloom. Max allowed himself to indulge, and if he wasn't already drunk on alcohol, he'd be intoxicated by *her*. Her taste, her smell, her response—everything about her enchanted him, and he couldn't get enough. God help him, but he was completely lost.

Suddenly, sobriety prevailed. *She betrayed me. She's playing me. And I'm letting her do it knowingly this time.*

"Fuck." The curse flew forcefully from his lips as he tore his mouth away from hers, angry with himself. "What the hell am I doing? I must have some kind of secret masochistic tendencies."

Mia squirmed out from under him, getting to her feet and leaving him laid out on the couch on his stomach, white spots starting to form in front of his eyes.

Either the couch is twirling, or I'm really wasted.

"I think you need coffee," she said quietly, walking away and into the kitchen.

"I need you," he whispered huskily, knowing she couldn't hear him, and feeling more lonely and abandoned than he'd ever felt in his life. Closing his eyes from the pain he was feeling, all he could think of were the things Kade and Travis had revealed before he'd left to find Mia.

She had to leave...
There was this boyfriend...
She was at Gran's house in Montana, and I think that's where she is now...
She never meant to hurt you...
Yeah, I helped her disappear...

The last comment had come from Travis, and Max hadn't been able to keep himself from trying to throttle the bastard. With the conversation still droning in his muddled mind, he gave in to the darkness that was threatening to consume him. It would give him a brief period of time in which he didn't need to think.

Being grateful for some sort of mercy, Max promptly passed out.

"Max?" Mia poked him experimentally, and then a little harder when he didn't respond. Sitting the cup of strong coffee on the end table, she fished in his pocket for his keys and went outside to the sporty little vehicle he had apparently rented. Opening the door, she immediately saw the partial bottle of whiskey sitting on the passenger seat.

"Not enough to kill him, but he's going to have a pretty horrible hangover in the morning," she mused, speaking aloud, stunned when something hurtled toward her. A sudden impact with the projectile nearly put her on her ass in the dirt.

"Tucker," she gasped with surprise, removing his paws from her chest and cuddling him when he had all four paws on the front seat. The hound gave her a disapproving look, but he licked her hand as she scratched him, his chubby body shuddering with delight.

After the canine had gotten enough affection, he jumped down and sniffed at the ground to do his business, acting like he wasn't entirely sure he liked his new surroundings.

"Come," Mia told Tucker affectionately, taking him into the house and closing the door behind her.

Tucker went immediately to Max's prone body, sniffing him first, and then positioning himself on the floor right beside the couch, shooting Mia an admonishing look.

"He's drunk. I didn't do it. I wasn't there. Why didn't you stop him?" she said defensively, and then laughed at herself for having a conversation with her dog and accusing the animal of negligence.

Mia plucked the cup of coffee intended for Max from the table and seated herself in a recliner, wondering why Max had brought Tucker with him. For a man who insisted that he and the dog didn't like each other, they certainly seemed bonded.

She sipped the hot coffee, watching Max sleep, his eyebrows drawn together as though he were frowning while he slumbered.

As long as she'd known him, she'd never seen Max have more than one drink. He never did anything to excess, and that included not drinking more than he could handle. What had prompted him to drink that way?

Maybe he had felt he needed it to be able to look at me again.

Mia cringed, fairly certain she was the reason for Max's sudden binge. Why else would he have to slug a ton of cheap whiskey at the end of the drive?

"He hates me, Tucker," she whispered softly to her dog, getting only what looked like a nod from her canine as he cocked his head. "And he thinks I had another man."

Maybe it was best for Max to think that she had betrayed him that way so he would hate her completely, but she had to wonder what her brothers had told him. She'd tried Travis' office phone and Kade's cell while she had been making coffee, still with no response.

I want to hate you, but I fucking can't.

Max's words played over and over in her mind, but she knew that had been the alcohol talking. Every word, every action since he'd come through that door had been from severe intoxication. Nothing he said or did could be taken seriously. Still, that kiss…

"Mia," Max shouted, rolling over on the couch until he was on his back, thrashing like he was fighting demons in his sleep. "Come back," he muttered in a low, desperate voice.

Mia set her coffee on the table beside the recliner, went to the couch and sank to her knees. "Max?" She stroked over the bruises on his face softly, wincing as she smoothed the rapidly emerging purple and yellow areas under his eye. She nudged Tucker, getting him to grudgingly move over so she could take his place.

"Mia," he called out again, his voice getting more desperate.

"Wake up, Max. You're dreaming," she told him in a louder, sterner voice.

He sat straight up, his eyes coming open, blinking at the light as though it hurt his eyes. He looked around the room, his gaze finally landing on her face. "You're here," he said, sounding relieved.

Mia rose to her feet. "I'm here," she agreed, reaching her hand out to him.

She knew Max was completely stoned—his eyes glazed over—but it still made her heart surge as he reached out and took her hand with no hesitation at all, like he completely trusted her. "Where are we going?" he mumbled as he got unsteadily to his feet.

"I'm putting you to bed," she answered adamantly, determined to get him to a more comfortable place to sleep.

He grinned wolfishly at her. "No argument here," he said happily, his fingers grazing over the ring finger of her left hand. "You're wearing my ring. You found it."

Mia didn't want to tell him she'd never lost it. She'd left it behind, not certain what Travis' plan had been when he'd sent his men for her, and she wanted to try to stay completely unnoticeable. Max Hamilton wasn't the type of man to do anything lightly, and he'd bought her a beautiful ring with enough quality diamonds to make a person go blind. It definitely had bling, so she'd reluctantly and intentionally left it behind.

"I am. I love it," she answered truthfully, wanting to tell him it had rarely left her finger the whole time they'd been apart. But she didn't. She pulled on his hand, guiding him into her bedroom.

Stopping beside the bed, she nearly giggled at the way Max was swaying slightly, smiling a shit-eating grin she'd never seen on him before. It was naughty. It was hot.

And…he was drunk.

There was no way she was taking advantage of the situation, not to mention the fact that he was so hammered that he probably couldn't even get it up. She lifted his arms and tugged at the back of his t-shirt, unable to ignore the flex of his powerful biceps as he held his arms out while she pulled the shirt over his head. Her breath hitched as Max's muscular chest and sculpted abs became visible and she dropped the shirt to the floor, completely ambivalent as to where it landed. Her entire mouth went dry, and she tried desperately not to look anywhere but at his face as she fumbled with the metal button of his jeans.

I need to treat him like a child who needs my help right now. He isn't in his right mind.

She tried…she really did. But he was definitely not a child, and as her fingers encountered difficulty unzipping his jeans because of the massive bulge beneath her fingers, Max grinned.

"Having problems, sweetheart?" he asked, his sultry voice slightly slurred.

Stepping back, she instructed, "Take off your jeans."

He ran a hand slowly down his ripped abdomen in a sensual, slow slide. "I liked it better when you were doing it," he drawled in a low, sexy voice that nearly made Mia jump him, drunk or not.

He flipped the button open with one tug and slowly lowered the zipper.

So much for thinking he couldn't get hard in his intoxicated condition.

Max started pushing his jeans down, taking his boxers with them. She grabbed for the elastic of his underwear, keeping them on his hips as he peeled off the pants.

"Off," he insisted, yanking on the red and black striped boxers.

"On," she demanded. Hell. There was only so much a woman could take, and even in his current state, Max was one big mass of scorching hot male. She pushed hard on his chest, sending him off-balance so he landed on the bed.

He repositioned himself, crawling to the top of the bed and lounging back against her pillows. "I'm lonely," he grumbled, patting the place beside him on the bed.

Oh no. Hell no. She wasn't going to get into that bed.

"I love you," he said huskily. "Come here next to me. I miss you."

That note of vulnerability, the fact that he was letting himself be wide open to her even after she'd hurt him, broke her completely. Tears streamed down her cheeks as she looked at her husband, the man she'd fallen hopelessly in love with, asking for nothing more than for her presence. Yeah. Sure. He was befuddled, but his look was so unguarded and unprotected at the moment that it tore her heart from her chest.

She tried to mentally tick off things in her mind, focusing on what she needed to do to fix her situation, but it didn't work. Max was calling to her, and right at this moment he needed her, and she couldn't deny him.

He'll hate me tomorrow. He probably came to discuss the divorce and how to get it over with as quickly as possible. He needed tons of liquor just to have a conversation with me. He's messed up right now.

There was every reason to ignore him, but she couldn't. It could be the last time she ever touched him, and the temptation was too great to disregard. Kicking off her sneakers, she climbed up onto the bed and snuggled beside him, sighing as her fingers were met with warm skin. "I love you, too," she admitted, knowing he'd probably never remember any of this in the morning, and thinking that it was better if he didn't. But the words left her lips involuntarily, needing to tell him just one last time.

His warm, protective arms snaked around her and she rested her head on his shoulder, giving herself this time, this stolen moment, to enjoy the exhilaration she felt when she was with Max. Their relationship had never been comfortable, or mildly contented. For her, it had always been a heart-thumping roller coaster that never ended. Maybe if they had been married for years, together for decades, her emotions would have settled down, but she was doubtful. She hadn't given Max her heart; he had stolen it, the stubborn organ leaping from her chest and into his the moment they had met.

Crazy love.

The tension in Max's arms relaxed, but he never let go of her, even after he was asleep. Mia relaxed into him and sighed, trying to absorb every bit of him into her soul, trying to keep every sensation locked in her memory.

He could hate her tomorrow. By then, she'd be gone.

Chapter 9

"**M**ax! Where in the hell is my sister?"

The loud, masculine shout jolted Max out of his slumber, causing him to sit up in bed, before quickly dropping his head back on the pillows. Damn. His gut lurched and he swallowed, trying to make his head stop throbbing. It was like a sledgehammer was beating against his skull.

Blinking as he opened his eyes, two men came into focus, two angry-looking guys. It took him a moment to identify them both as Kade and Travis, his focus a little blurry.

He held up his hand weakly. "No screaming. My head is ready to explode." He winced as even his own voice exacerbated his slamming headache.

"Nobody was yelling," Kade replied, his voice laced with laughter. "Jesus Christ, you must have gotten pickled."

"Coffee and aspirin," Travis said calmly, turning and walking out of the room.

"You look like hell, buddy. What the hell happened? Where is Mia?" Kade questioned curiously.

Max closed his eyes, seeing only flashes of scenes from the night before. Were they real or imaginary? He had no fucking idea. All he knew was that he'd come to Montana like a raging maniac, to see a wife who had no desire to see *him*. "Is she gone?" He groaned as he tried to sit up, vaguely remembering getting into Mia's bed, or being put to bed by his wife. She'd better be here somewhere. He was getting damn sick and tired of chasing a woman who kept running away from him. What the hell was he thinking?

Truth was, he hadn't been thinking. He'd been running on anger and adrenaline. When he'd finally gotten to Mia's place in Montana, he'd questioned himself and his sanity. He'd nearly turned around and left, but after he'd taken several shots of that shitty whiskey, he'd decided they needed to have a talk—the reason why they'd need to have a discussion escaping him at the moment.

"Well, she's not here. And a truck that I assume is hers is still in the driveway." Kade shot him a disgruntled look.

"She had a rental car. She must have picked it up at the airport." Max remembered seeing the compact vehicle in the drive, parked next to an older truck.

"Then she's gone," Kade said remorsefully. "Damn it."

"I'll stay away from her. Maybe she'll stop running." Max was resigned. Mia couldn't seem to do anything *other* than run from him, so he needed to stop chasing her. It was rather pointless anyway.

"She isn't running from you, man. She's scared," Kade answered angrily.

"Of what?" Max asked, perplexed. He swung around and dropped his feet to the ground, shooting Kade a dubious glance.

"Long story that you need to hear. Take a shower, for God's sake. You smell like a damn distillery. Since when do you get drunk?" Kade stepped back, waving his hand in the air to get rid of the odor to make his point.

"Since your sister decided to leave me again for another man," Max shot back at Kade, irritation and what he assumed was a massive hangover trying his patience.

"We need to get one thing straight." Kade was shouting now. "My sister loves you. I have no idea why. Personally, I think you're a real asshole to wake up to, but she's obviously blind to that. She didn't leave you *for* another man. She left you *because* of one. There's a big difference. If you would have stayed to hear Travis out instead of trying to kill him, you'd know the truth by now. Take a shower and meet us in the living room before you piss me off and I take a shot at the other side of your face."

Max rarely saw Kade angry, so his brother-in-law's outrage took him by surprise. He watched Kade turn and walk out of the bedroom, leaving him alone with his thoughts and his hangover.

He found the adjoining bathroom with a shower, cleaning himself up as he pondered Kade's words. What the hell did it mean? Who or what was Mia afraid of…and why?

Feeling nearly human, he went to the living room, wearing the same jeans and t-shirt he'd worn the day before. He'd taken the time to cram a few things in a bag, but it was in the car.

Kade came out of the kitchen, carrying two mugs of coffee. Silently, he handed Max some aspirin, which he downed immediately, and then started on the coffee.

Travis was already sitting in one of the recliners, reading a newspaper with a cup of coffee in hand and Tucker sitting at his feet.

"Traitor," Max mumbled to the canine, slightly satisfied when he noticed that Travis looked as beat-up as he did.

He sat on the couch, silently slugging as much coffee as he could. Tucker gave him an apologetic look and came to sit at his feet.

Travis put his paper aside and Kade flopped into the other recliner, both brothers drilling him with a hostile expression.

"I don't know where she went. I did get drunk, and we…talked. She was here when I went to sleep," he stated flatly. "I don't know why she left and I don't know where she went. She ran. Again. It's something Mia seems to excel at doing. I assume there was no note this time?"

"Nothing. How much do you remember?" Kade asked, his expression relaxing to an only slightly contrary look.

"Not a lot," Max answered honestly. "I remember her being here when I went to sleep. I have a few empty spaces in my memory of last night. I'm not sure what was real and what I imagined." And he hated it. No wonder he'd never gotten completely plastered.

"Welcome to 'the morning after,' Mr. Perfect," Kade said evilly. "I just wish I could have been here to see it. The 'always in control Max Hamilton' three sheets to the wind? I would have paid good money for that show."

"No reruns. It was an exclusive showing," Max grumbled, swearing he'd never get that drunk again. The next morning wasn't worth it. He felt like he been chewed up and spit out by some kind of mythological monster with razor-sharp teeth. "Tell me about Mia." His mind was on only one thing at the moment, and that was his wayward wife. "Is she safe?"

"I have a team of investigators tracking her as we speak. I should have a location on her shortly. She's obviously headed back to the airport. She hired the rental she got from there and there aren't many other means of transport away from here." Travis spoke for the first time. His voice was well modulated and restrained, speaking as though he were in a business meeting. The only telling thing was his eyes, his usually glacial look expressing untamed emotion. "To make a long story short, she got involved in a bad relationship back when she was in college. The asshole finally got put in jail and we thought it was over. He got out of prison right before Mia disappeared the first time, threatening to kill you, Kade, and me if she didn't come back to him. She was afraid…and I helped her. She's my sister. Her safety was my main concern."

"She was my goddamn wife. Why didn't you tell me? I could have protected her," Max answered angrily, ready to pound Travis all over again.

"You were unavailable. In fact, Danny had Mia in his grasp when your plane took off, your head in the sight of a rifle and ready to blow your head off. Your wife saved your life," Travis answered casually. "Danny Harvey was a career criminal, completely insane, and ready to do whatever it took to get Mia back. He was also a sharpshooter who could pick off a target at long distances. He won a lot of competitions when he was young. He rarely missed a target."

"Why was Mia even with him? She couldn't have loved someone like that," Max asked harshly.

Kade answered. "She was twenty-one years old, had an old man who was a raging alcoholic and completely insane. He beat his wife and children often and repeatedly. Mia suffered under my father's hand. We all did. Do you really think she even knew what love was? Do you think she knew what normal was?" Kade leaned forward in the chair, his fists clenched. "I was gone, you were gone, and Travis was the only thing standing between her and him. I was pissed off, too, Max, when I found out he'd been responsible for hiding her. But I might have done the same damn thing if it meant keeping Mia safe."

"You should have told me. I thought she was dead." Max still wasn't convinced. She was his wife, dammit. "All those years, I fucking grieved for her."

"It wasn't a picnic for her either. Do you think she wanted to go? She was terrified he'd kill you. She ran to keep you safe. She didn't give a shit about what happened to her. I can testify to that because I saw the way he messed her up." Travis' voice was heated. "Back in college and before she disappeared."

"You knew when she was in college?" Max questioned resentfully.

"Not immediately. She went to Virginia to go to college. My father wanted her to go to business school in Florida and get involved in the business, but that wasn't what Mia wanted. Gran made jewelry when she was alive, and that's what Mia wanted to do. Mia had this house and her trust as an inheritance, but she didn't have control of anything yet. She had to bury herself in student loans that she could pay back later to attend the college in Virginia that had the BFA and MFA that she wanted to become a jewelry designer." Travis released an audible breath, pausing for a moment before continuing, "Kade and I were both in school too, but once I finished my business degree and was working, I decided to go to Virginia to surprise Mia. I ended up more surprised than she was when I saw what was happening to her." Travis' voice cracked, a slight dent in his emotional shield.

"What happened?" Max asked stoically, not at all sure he wanted to know. But he needed to hear it. "Did he hurt her?"

"Yeah," Travis confessed. "Pretty badly right about the time I went to visit. But even through all that bullshit, she was working part-time and pulling excellent grades. She was about ready to enter her master's program. And he was trying to convince her not to—with his fists. He didn't want her accumulating more loans. The bastard wanted plenty of that trust fund left when she was able to get to it."

"Fuck!" Max exploded, so enraged he wanted to kill the guy. How could any man hurt Mia? "How did she separate herself from him?"

"She didn't have to. He went to jail. I think she'd been trying to get away from the relationship for a while, but he really did a number on her," Travis answered, setting his coffee mug on the table, and leaning back in his chair, crossing his arms in front of him.

"What were the charges?" Max asked, his eyes narrowing as he looked at Travis, reading something unsaid.

"Assault with a deadly weapon. Nasty ordeal," Travis replied, deadpan.

"You set him up," Max guessed, fairly certain Travis was the man who had put the asshole in jail.

"I went to have a discussion with him. Let's just say I made sure there were witnesses."

"Did Mia know?" Max was enraged, his mind flashing with scenarios of Mia hurting, Mia crying, Mia bleeding.

"No," Travis answered calmly. "She had her studies and her job to worry about. All she ever knew was that he was going to jail, and she was safe. It was all she needed to know."

Max barely noticed when Kade got up and took the empty mug from his hand. He let go, his hand shaking with pent-up rage as he released the handle. "And last time?" Max rasped, spearing Travis with a resentful stare.

"He took her by surprise when she was leaving her car in a parking lot. She had dismissed your security, telling them she was going to be with Kade and me, and had our security. She told them to take some time off because she didn't want them following her around town on errands. Danny had her in his vehicle before she even realized what happened. It was the morning you left, and he took her to an area near your jet, forced her to watch while he showed her how easily he could kill you," Travis explained, picking his coffee mug up from the table and taking a sip of his coffee, scowling as he realized it was now cold.

"She's a smart woman. She told him she would go with him, gave him everything he wanted to hear, but she said she needed a day to take care of some things first. She finally convinced him to let her go by herself by telling him she needed to arrange things to get to her trust fund. Somehow, she convinced him to meet her the next morning, making him think she wanted to go with him. I don't think she wanted to even tell me, but she asked for my help and I wasn't going to refuse her. We set up the stuff at the beach, hoping she would be assumed dead, and I got her away from Tampa as fast as I could. I wanted to tell you, Max. And I wanted Kade to know she was alive. I just wasn't entirely sure how either of you would react. I couldn't risk leaving any trail to Mia. This man was psychotic, probably more deranged than my father and a hundred times more dangerous. I wanted her safe and needed time to track his ass down. I never realized that it would take over two years to find the bastard," Travis grumbled.

"What about the police?" Max asked, already fairly certain he knew the answer. He'd dealt with the police himself on Mia's case, and he was doubtful he would have wanted to give Danny that kind of time to take Mia away.

Kade walked back into the living room, handing Max a full mug of coffee as he answered, "Our father was a nut case. Do you have any idea how many times the police were at our house for a domestic dispute, usually reported by neighbors? The Harrison family was notorious, and not in a good way. Do you really think they would have taken her seriously? They would have done their job, but it would have alerted Danny, and it probably wouldn't have stopped him. There isn't a lot they can do with stalkers."

"But he hurt her," Max argued, having problems even speaking those words.

"No witnesses. No proof that he was to blame. They wouldn't have had any evidence to immediately arrest him. Do you really think we could be totally certain that she was safe?" Travis drawled bitterly. "I'm sorry, Max. But I wasn't taking that chance with my baby sister or Kade. She needed to disappear for a while until I could track him down. Had I known the bastard was getting out of prison early, I would have had him tailed."

"For over two fucking years? You should have told me. She was my wife to protect."

"She was my sister before she was your wife," Travis pointed out gruffly.

"I didn't know," Max answered, his statement haunted and hollow. "She never told me. I should have known she was in danger. I should have known about *him*."

Did I ever open myself up to her? Did she think she really had reason to trust me not to judge her? She was trying to be the perfect wife, trying to please me.

"You're not psychic, buddy," Kade replied. "She obviously didn't want to talk about it. I never knew either. And he had been in jail for years. Nobody could predict what he was going to do when he got out."

"I was busy running away from how I felt about her, and she was trying to make herself into a perfect wife. It wasn't all her fault. I wasn't exactly accessible. I wasn't really 'seeing' her," Max admitted, knowing it was true. Mia was his one and only, but they'd spent two years dancing around each other, both trying to be what the other expected them to be. In some ways, they had been close, shared a lot of things, but none of the important stuff. Neither one of them had been ready to share the gut-wrenching, emotional things that they really should have talked about, helped each other through.

"And if you *had* seen her?" Kade asked grimly.

Max shrugged. "I would have loved her the same way. But I might have been able to allow her to be who she was and not try to please me. Maybe I would have pulled my head out of my ass long enough to realize that she needed me too."

The heavy silence between the three men was suddenly broken as music started pounding from the general vicinity of Travis' hip. Max looked up in surprise as Travis dug into the front pocket of his pants to silence the upbeat, trendy song.

"Damn secretary has been playing with my phone again," he mumbled, punching the button on the smartphone to answer it as he stood and walked toward the kitchen to take the call.

"Don't blame Travis," Kade requested quietly. "Growing up with my father wasn't easy, and he was trying to protect Mia. We grew up trying to protect her from my father. Travis might have been a bit misguided, but Mia begged him not to tell anyone. She was afraid for all of us."

"I don't. Much," Max admitted, both to Kade and to himself. "I should have known more about her past, protected her myself. But that bastard is mine. He's dead," he warned Kade, his eyes lethal.

"He's already dead," Kade replied flatly. "That's why we've been trying to talk to Mia. When she lost her memory, obviously Travis couldn't say anything. But he needed her to know that Danny's dead. She's on the run because she doesn't know. She's still trying to protect us. I know she left that note and ran again to try to protect you. She loves you, Max. If you don't understand anything else, you have to know that."

"The guy is dead. Was it Travis?" Max questioned, really pissed now that he'd never have the chance to make the bastard breathe his last.

Kade shrugged nonchalantly, like his brother killed people every day. "He won't admit it. He says he finally tracked Danny down in Colorado and went to have a talk with him." He quirked an eyebrow at Max as he continued, "We know exactly what kind of 'talks' Travis would have when someone threatens his family. He says Danny fled before he could even get his hands on him. Travis got in his car and chased him down some winding mountain road and Danny made a fatal driving error. Danny's car went over the side of the mountain.

Travis confirmed he was dead before he sent his guys to escort Mia back home."

Fatal driving error? Hell, Travis had been a professional racecar driver before he'd focused his attention on his father's business. The asshole had never had a chance. Travis could make maneuvers that would make other guys piss themselves in fear. "Travis outmaneuvered him," Max stated aloud.

Kade smirked. "You think?"

"I'm glad the bastard is dead. I just regret not having a chance at him myself. I'd tear his fucking head off for hurting Mia."

Kade's smile grew broader. "You know, you get less and less like Mr. Perfect every day. You're starting to sound pretty brutal. What happened to the calm, smooth, and completely controlled Max Hamilton?"

"Never had any control when it comes to Mia. She makes me crazy," Max rumbled, slamming his empty coffee mug on the table in front of him a lot harder than necessary. "Why didn't Travis contact her once Danny was dead and tell her?"

"He had agents keeping an eye on her. He tried to call a few times after Danny died, but she didn't answer. They hadn't had any contact since she left. He sent her money in a convoluted way so nobody could track it, money that she barely touched the whole time she was here. Travis didn't want anyone to link the two of them together in any way. This house was left to Mia by Gran, along with her funds in trust, but I know I didn't even think about it. Did you?" When Max shook his head reluctantly, Kade continued, "Travis sent his guys in to pick Mia up when he couldn't reach her by phone and bring her home. He wanted to meet her at the jet to tell her, but he had some critical meeting that he couldn't get out of. When he got home, she wasn't there. She must have got to his place and left for the park almost immediately."

"Why was she there? Did she know we'd be there?" Max asked quietly, wondering why Mia had come directly to the park that day.

"I'm not sure. My guess is she saw the invitation from Sam on Travis' cupboard. He said it was in the kitchen on the table when he got home." Kade frowned as he finished, "It's the only thing that makes sense. Her shorter hair and the hair color were probably things she did before she left Montana. She didn't know Danny was dead and probably wanted to keep a low profile."

"She came for me," Max said huskily, the thought slamming him in the gut, hope starting to bloom. "She knew I would probably be there since Sam was hosting the picnic."

"Nah…I think she was looking for me," Kade replied with a laugh, chuckling even louder as Max shot him a hostile look. "Or maybe not, since she was staring at you with a nauseatingly lovesick look."

"She seemed…different after the accident. Still Mia, but more…" Max wasn't quite sure how to explain it so he finished, "whole." He was still kicking himself in the ass for never noticing that she had needed him earlier. He'd been too busy running away to realize that she was twisting herself in knots and needed reassurance as much as he did.

"I don't think it was the accident that changed her. She went through counseling while she was here in Montana. It was her deal with Travis. He made her promise she'd find someone to talk to, try to heal," Kade told Max quietly. "I think maybe it helped. I didn't get to see her often because I was on the road so much after I started college, but she seemed different to how she had been when she was younger. Like she was more comfortable in her own skin."

Travis strode out of the kitchen, pocketing his cell phone as he said, "She's at the airport. She bought herself a one-way ticket to Los Angeles."

"What the hell for?" Max asked belligerently.

"She's on the run. It's a big city," Travis surmised. "She's going to try to get lost in a crowd."

"When? Do you have the info?" There was no way Mia was flying away from him. "What time is it?"

Kade wasn't wearing a watch and he looked at Travis. "I didn't bring my cell."

Travis pulled up the long sleeve of his casual shirt and glanced at his Rolex. "It's nine. Her flight leaves at eleven thirty."

Max was already on his feet. "I've got this. You two can go home. It's time for my wife and me to come to an understanding," he said menacingly. "No more interference," he warned Travis, spearing him with a warning glance.

Travis walked to Max, holding out his hand. "Agreed. Don't ever hurt her, and I won't have to kill you. She's been through enough, Max. Make her happy."

Max looked from Travis to Kade, suddenly realizing that all three siblings had been through hell. Maybe Mia would tell him more than the bare minimum about her life growing up if he gave her the chance. Her past had influenced her when she was younger, but it hadn't broken her. Max gripped Travis' hand and shook it. "Thanks for messing up my face."

Travis smirked. "Likewise."

At that moment, he and Travis had reached an understanding, a man-to-man agreement that neither one would ever break.

"I'll change clothes in the car." Max snatched his keys from his front pocket and raced toward the door. He needed to at least throw on a clean shirt. He'd showered, but he must have spilled some drops of whiskey on the front of the shirt he had on. He could still smell it.

"Need a clean shirt?" Kade asked cheerfully. "I have extras."

Max rolled his eyes as he opened the door, looking at Kade's blinding orange florescent shirt. He wasn't quite sure what the blobs of gray and black were dotting the surface, but he thought they were fish…or sharks.

"Hell no. I do want her to actually come back to me," he told his brother-in-law bluntly, closing the door behind him.

"Hey…Mia loves my shirts," Max heard Kade yell through the door as he raced for his vehicle.

The smell of alcohol assailed him as he closed the door of his rented vehicle, and it wasn't coming from just the garment he was wearing. Grabbing the bottle, he lowered the window and tossed it onto the dirt driveway. He'd throw it away when he got back. Mia was coming home with him, and she was intoxicating enough to keep him drunk on her forever. The liquor had been a poor substitute, and it had fogged part of his memory. From this day forward, he wanted to remember everything, experience every part of the woman he loved.

Starting the car, he jammed it roughly into gear and turned the small sports car around, heading down the driveway much faster than he should be going down a road full of potholes. But Max ignored them, his mind already focused on only one goal.

No more bullshit.

No more games.

Mia belonged to him, and it was beyond time he claimed her completely, knew her totally, loved her unconditionally. And once he found her, he was never letting go.

Chapter 10

Mia fastened her seatbelt woodenly, her entire body exhausted, her heart and soul empty. She might be here on this plane bound for Los Angeles, but she was only a shell, a body going to another place. Her heart had stayed with Max back at the ranch.

She stowed her purse and carry-on beneath the seat of the aircraft and leaned her head back against the headrest, closing her eyes against the pain of knowing that she was leaving Max. Again. Maybe taking those few hours in the shelter of his arms had been a mistake, making it even more painful to be without him. Somehow, she needed to rebuild her life away from everyone she cared about. She was toxic to them, and if Danny did locate her, she didn't want anyone she loved to be anywhere nearby.

"You have to the count of ten to get that beautiful ass up and out of this plane."

Mia's eyes popped open in shock, the sound of Max's deep, masculine voice vibrating right next to her ear, so close she could feel his warm breath caress her temple.

"Max?" She stared right into his eyes, stormy, turbulent, and so close she had to tilt her head back to see them. "You have to get off this plane. We're going to be taking off soon."

"One." Both his expression and voice were uncompromising.

"Max. Stop this. You need to go." Mia was panicked. Max didn't look like he was about to back down, and she couldn't get off this plane. But she wanted to. God, how she wanted to leave right now, throw herself into Max's safe embrace and let him take her wherever he wanted to go.

"Two." He bent down and snagged her carry-on from under the seat and dropped her purse in her lap.

He brushed his upper body against her, and Mia tried not to inhale the masculine fragrance that assaulted her as he straightened.

Mentally slapping herself, she remembered that she couldn't be weak. "I'm leaving you, Max. I don't want to be with you anymore. I don't love you." *Liar.* She was such a liar. But she couldn't think of any other way to make him back off. And she really, really needed him to go. She couldn't look him in the eye and say that she didn't love him, so she stared straight ahead, waiting for him to exit the plane.

"Three."

Mia's eyes snapped back to his face. He'd slung her small bag over his shoulder and his arms were folded in front of him. He looked obstinate, and determined to get her off the plane. And at the moment, Max Hamilton looked anything but tame. In fact, he looked pretty damn certain he was going to bend her to his will.

Okay…well…she could be just as pigheaded as he was being at the moment. "I'm not going, Max." She crossed her arms, frowning.

"Four." He reached down and flipped the latch on her seatbelt, opening it with a simple flick of his wrist.

"Don't make this harder than it already is. Please." Mia had lost all desire for pretense, her look beseeching him to cease. Blinking hard, trying to keep her tears of frustration from falling, she saw a dangerous glint in his eyes, a dogged stubbornness that warned her that he wasn't going to relent.

"Ten." The word had barely left Max's lips before he snatched her bodily out of her seat and slung her over his shoulder.

Mia scrambled to hang onto her purse, her fists beating on Max's back. "Let go. Dammit. What are you doing?" It was actually pretty obvious that he was bodily carrying her off the plane, his stride steady and even, as though he were trying not to jostle her around too much.

Mia decided at that moment that there was nothing more mortifying than being bodily removed from a full aircraft. Luckily, she was near the front of the plane, but Max never stopped to let her down, even after they'd exited and were heading down the ramp and into the main airport.

Exasperated, she said to his back, "What happened to counting to ten?"

"Took too long. You talked too much," he answered abruptly, moving toward the airport exit, drawing looks from the people they were passing that ranged from amusement to alarm.

Max had parked in the loading zone, a completely illegal place to leave his car. "I bet I would have gotten a ticket," she mumbled, irritated.

By the time he deposited her in the bucket seat of the sporty vehicle, she was shaking with frustration. He didn't say a word as he calmly snapped her seatbelt, closed the passenger door and then jogged around to the driver's side. He had the car in motion before she could get out, which she realized had been his intention.

"You do understand that you just kidnapped me. Last I knew, it's illegal to take a woman without her permission," she told him in a sharp tone. "How did you get through security, anyway?"

Max shrugged. "I bought a ticket on the flight."

For a man who'd been completely drunk the night before, he looked pretty unaffected by the amount of alcohol he'd consumed. He handled the little sports car with confidence, steadily making his way to the freeway. "I do not want to go back to the ranch. I need to be on that plane."

"No you don't," Max answered with irritating certainty. "Danny's dead. And you're never running away from me again. I'll make sure to give you every reason to stay."

Danny's dead? Max knows about Danny? He knows—he has to—and he still came for me. Why?

Mia's entire body suddenly relaxed, her panic completely deflated. "How do you know about him?"

"Travis," Max answered with more than a little irritation in his voice. "Why didn't you ever tell me, Mia?"

"I thought it was all over, and I wanted to leave it in the past. I didn't think you'd understand a woman being that stupid. What did Travis tell you?" she asked quietly. *It's over. It's really over.* The reality that a man she had feared for so long was finally gone forever hadn't quite sunk in for her.

"He told me everything. Your relationship in college and the abuse, Danny nearly killing me, you saving my life. And you are not stupid. Did Travis miss anything?" Max turned onto the freeway, glancing at her briefly with a frown.

"It's over," Mia whispered, wrapping her arms around herself, afraid to believe it was really true. She looked over at Max, studying his profile as she tried to make herself accept that she didn't have to run anymore. Would Max ever forgive her now that he knew the whole truth? Or would he be repulsed?

I've dealt with those emotions. I'm not the woman I was two years ago. Maybe not, but she had to fight her insecurities where Max was concerned. There were some things she hadn't told him, things he had a right to know.

"Your running days are over, sweetheart, but you and me...we'll never be over," Max told her dangerously. "Not unless you've really stopped loving me, and you really want it to be over."

"But the woman you fell in love with doesn't exist. She never really did," Mia told him honestly.

"For me she did and she still does." Max glanced over at her with a look of fierce possessiveness that made Mia practically melt into a puddle on the seat of the car. "I didn't care about the superficial things. It didn't matter what you wore, what you said to other people, or what was in your past. I fell in love with you, the you who was always there and still is, no matter how much you twisted yourself to fit an image I never really cared about." Max turned off the exit for the ranch before adding, "I want to know everything about you now. Maybe it was my fault because I put you on a pedestal instead of treating you like my woman. I thought you were perfect, but I would have felt that way regardless. Even if I'd known about your past, your insecurities, your personal preferences, I still would have fucking worshipped the ground you walked on."

"Why?" she asked curiously. "I was a screwed-up woman who put up with a highly abusive relationship for over a year. My self-confidence was nil, and I never felt like I was good enough for you, or enough of a woman to keep you."

Max pulled into the driveway of the ranch as he answered, "I can't be the same man I was before either, Mia. The love was real, but we were both pretending, hiding."

"What now?" she whispered softly.

Reaching the end of the long driveway, Max stopped the car in front of the ranch house and turned to her. "Now I plan to show my wife exactly how I feel about her, love her the way I've always loved her but was too afraid to show it. We trust each other instead of running away. We strip each other bare in more ways than one." His voice was bold, but still held a touch of vulnerability.

"I trust you. I always have. It was myself who I didn't trust," she answered, mesmerized by the covetous look in his eyes and the fierceness of his expression.

Time seemed to stop, both of them staring at each other with unrestrained passion, and there wasn't a sound except for their harsh breathing to break the silence.

"Fuck. I need you," Max finally said harshly. He opened the door of the car and grabbed her bag. He was on the other side of the vehicle before Mia could even unbuckle her seatbelt, her fingers trembling as she fumbled with the restraint.

Max flipped it open and she stumbled out of the car, landing in his arms. He picked her up and strode to the house. "Key," he requested impatiently.

"In the plant. I can see it. Were Kade and Travis here?" she asked breathlessly.

"Yeah."

"They didn't even bother to hide it."

Max fished the key from the plant beside the door and unlocked the door, pushing it open with his foot. Dropping the key on the table next to the door, he released his hold on her bag and set her on her feet. "I want you naked right now. I need you wanting me and moaning my name. I want to feel every emotion you have while I fuck you until you're satisfied."

"B-Bedroom," she stammered, her body yearning to be joined with his, the desire so raw and carnal that her entire being was trembling and the moist heat between her thighs felt almost unbearable.

"I'm not going to make it that far." Max growled, the feral, reverberating sound vibrating low and dangerously in the air as he grabbed the edges of her shirt and popped every button off the Western button-down she was wearing. "Mine. Every damn inch of you is mine."

Mia drew in a sharp breath as Max lowered his head and fused his mouth to hers. His kiss was possessive and punishing, but Mia welcomed it. She wanted to be completely branded and taken, declared his in the most primitive way possible.

Crazy love.

The way she felt about Max was insane and volatile, and she couldn't care less if he could feel every wild emotion that coursed through her body, because she was simply answering his call. He felt the same way. They shared the same lush primitive fury that was ready to combust at any moment.

She opened to him, surrendered to him, entwining her tongue with his as she pushed her hands beneath his t-shirt and inwardly sighed as she touched warm skin over steely muscle. Trying to touch him everywhere at once, her hands roamed over his chest and around his back, her fingers touching every hot inch she could get to, and finding nothing except unyielding strength.

The button on her jeans popped and the zipper came down. Max tore his mouth from hers, his breathing ragged as he tugged the shirt off her arms and tore open the clasp of her bra, the undergarment hitting the floor seconds later, joining her discarded top. Mia clawed at Max's shirt, desperate to get him just as naked, but he ignored her, his complete focus on tugging the jeans down her legs, taking her panties with them.

Grabbing her hand, he led her to the couch and bent her over the elevated arm. She braced her hands on the cushion to steady herself, her breathing so hot and heavy that she was gasping, her red-hot need for Max making her come undone.

His palms gripped the cheeks of her ass, alternately cupping and caressing each one reverently. "Never run from me again," he demanded harshly, his breathing ragged. "We belong together."

Feeling his need to assert his claim and have her under his control, she murmured quietly, "Do it. I know you want to." Everything feminine inside her responded to his dominance, moisture rushing heatedly between her thighs. "Do it."

Max was right. She did belong with him, and to him, and she wanted him to claim her. She knew exactly what he needed right now, and she was squirming to feel the sting of his palm on her ass, an erotic pleasure that, coming from Max, would drive her completely mad.

"I can't," he answered, frustrated.

Mia knew why he was hesitating. "I know the difference between abuse and love play. For God's sake, do it. And make me come," she ordered him, unable to wait another moment.

"I'm not exactly playing," Max hissed softly but dangerously.

His palm connected with her ass solidly, jolting her body and making her skin tingle with erotic pain and pleasure. It hurt, but the excitement of Max letting loose his dominant tendencies on her far outweighed the sting of his palm.

She wanted more…

And she got what she wanted.

The second and third impacts of his hand on her ass went straight to her core, the muscles clenching, begging for release.

Moaning aloud at the forth smack, she begged, "Please, Max. Make me come."

Her ass was stinging and her clit was throbbing for attention.

"Never leave me again, Mia. Not for any reason," Max warned, his hand caressing her stinging cheeks and delving between her thighs. "Promise me."

The masculine, commanding tone of his voice sent a shiver down her spine.

"Touch me. Please," she begged, desperate.

He teased her clit lightly, just enough to make her want to scream. Her entire body was one big mass of tangled heat and desire, ready to explode, and only Max held the power to make her detonate.

He smacked her ass again, followed by a caress to her cheeks and then a delicate teasing between her thighs. "Promise me," he insisted, continuing the same pattern over and over.

Unable to speak, she moaned aloud, clawing at the leather of the couch cushion. Max was ramping up her need to implosion level, and she wasn't sure she wanted it to stop, but her tolerance was at an end. "Yes. I promise. I love you."

"I love you too," he answered harshly.

His fingers slid between her saturated folds, finding her engorged, sensitive bud and gliding over it with persistent pressure. The pleasure was so heady, intensified by her stinging rear, so intoxicating that her legs trembled and a strangled cry left her lips as release rushed forward at a dizzying speed.

"Come for me, sweetheart," he coaxed. "You're so hot, so wet. Let go. I'll catch you when you fall."

Mia did let go, with an orgasm that shattered her whole body, pieces of herself scattering everywhere as she rode the climax, whimpering and moaning incoherently as Max buried two fingers inside her, keeping the pressure on her clit with his thumb as she came, challenging her to take every bit of pleasure she could handle, plus a little more.

Max did catch her, just as he promised he would, wrapping a muscular arm around her waist to keep her steady, holding her while she came down gasping, her heart racing at insane gallop inside her chest.

Mia had no idea how much time had passed as she floated back down to earth. Max was holding her with one arm, while the fingers of his other hand were lightly stroking the curve at the top of her left buttock.

"What's this?" Max asked roughly, his fingers tracing over a pattern at the top of her butt cheek.

He was fingering her tattoo.

Out of the corner of her eye, she saw Max's t-shirt hit the carpet. She regretted not seeing him remove it with what had to have been a sexy, one-handed removal that probably would have made her salivate.

"You," she answered honestly. "A red rose for true love, and your name." The tattoo was small and delicate, a red rose in full bloom, tiny and detailed with simply the word *Max* written underneath.

She'd desperately wanted to carry Max with her forever, and it was the only thing she could think of that would brand her as his for the rest of her life.

"Holy fuck!" The curse sounded strangled and raw when it sprang from Max's lips. He gripped her hips tightly, his thumb still stroking over the marking as he filled her with one smooth stroke.

Yes. Yes. Yes. Mia needed this joining more than she needed her next breath. His cock stretched her as the smooth walls of her channel clenched him tightly. Still, she pressed back against his body, desperate and greedy to have him and keep him inside her.

"You marked yourself for me, to be mine," Max rasped.

"Had to," she gasped. "Needed something. Anything." She nearly sobbed as Max's hips moved back, pulling his cock almost completely out of her and thrusting back in with a low groan.

Leaning down, stretching his chest against her back, he nipped at her shoulder and then laved it with his tongue, working his way slowly up the side of her neck and finally whispered huskily into her ear. "That's the hottest thing I've ever seen. My name branded on you forever. Does that make me a sick bastard?" He flicked his tongue over her earlobe, making her shake with desire. "I want to stay just like this forever. My cock inside you, my body entwined with yours, surrounded by you. Nothing has ever felt this good." His hands cupped her breasts, his fingers squeezing her nipples and then stroking over them in a soothing motion. The pleasure/pain of the erotic motions made her pant with need, her whole body quivering.

Mia turned her head and his lips ravished hers, the awkward angle making it difficult for her to return his embrace. But Max didn't seem to mind. He ravished her lips with his tongue, tasting her like she was the most delicious thing on earth. His tongue entered and retreated, making her hips flex back, needing that same motion inside her.

"I can't wait," he groaned as he released her mouth, his sharp, heavy breaths bathing the tender skin of her neck with heat. "I *need* to fuck you."

The raw oath coming from Max made her clench around him. The fact that she made him so needy was empowering and humbling. She could bring this proud, strong, masculine, sexy man to his knees, but that was the last thing she wanted. Max had her—heart, body, and soul—and all she wanted to do was sink into him, let him be the dominant male that he needed to be with her. And the honest truth was...she craved it. "Then do it," she told him softly. "Please. I need it, too."

Max straightened and gripped her hips tightly, and she moaned in relief as he started to move, his cock mastering her, thrusting in and out of her with powerful strokes.

Everything about the fierce coupling aroused her. Max's bold thrusts, his groin slapping against her still-burning ass cheeks, the sounds of their groans mingling together all filled her with an incendiary heat that just spiraled upward until she was completely lost. She felt nothing except Max and their frenzied rush to meld together.

"I love you, Mia. I love you so goddamn much it hurts," Max choked out with a tortured groan, gripping her hips and pumping into her with a desperation that was nearly palpable. Tension spiraled in the air, both of them panting, sweating. Mia's entire body was perspiring, and she could see droplets of moisture from her face hitting the brown leather of the couch.

And then...she saw nothing...as she closed her eyes, throwing her head back with a scream of pleasure as her climax hit her with an intensity that made her arms give way, her head dropping to the arm of the couch. She was rendered helpless as her channel convulsed wildly around Max's hammering cock.

"Christ," Max cursed, his body tensing as his heated release flooded her with warmth. His sweaty body lowered to hers, and his arms encircled her protectively. He buried his face in her hair, murmuring incoherent, tender words as he recovered his breath. Mia went limp, knowing Max would keep her safe, unable to move.

They stayed just like that, lost in a world that contained only the two of them and their out-of-control emotions. Finally, Max disconnected them and swung her into his arms. He kicked out of the jeans that he obviously hadn't bothered to remove completely, and dropped onto the couch, taking her with him, holding her tightly on his lap.

Mia finally got to drown in his beautiful hazel eyes as she looked up at him, his face still radiating a ferocious possessiveness that made her shiver with pleasure. Being loved like this by the man who was everything to her was all she'd ever wanted, all she'd ever needed. Finally, she felt free, and it was an incredible feeling. She could be exactly who she was and Max would love her.

She put her arms around his neck and pulled his lips to hers, giving him a tender, emotional embrace that made her feel like after all these years, she'd finally come home.

Chapter 11

"I guess we really should have talked before we did…um… that," Mia remarked casually as she looked adoringly up at her husband. "We both have questions."

Max grinned wickedly. "How we just communicated was incredible for me. I think talking is highly overrated." He stroked over her tattoo before adding, "I can't believe you marked yourself with my name."

Mia shrugged, not understanding why he'd be surprised. "I missed you so much that I had to do something or go crazy. I wanted something permanent to somehow keep you close to me. Maybe that sounds crazy, 'cause I never thought I'd tattoo your name on my ass, but I wanted it."

Max's smile grew broader. "It looks good on you. I would have never asked you to do it because I know it hurts. But it's sexy as hell. I'll never look at it and not want to fuck you right that minute. So you better cover it up unless you want to be taken the second I see it."

"Then I guess I'm going to be walking away from you naked a lot," she said, smiling as she started to wonder if there would ever be a time that she didn't want Max all over her.

"Funny thing, though..." he started and then trailed off, looking like he was contemplating something.

"What?" she asked curiously.

Max gently moved her from his lap to sit beside him. He turned his back to her and simply said, "This. I got it a few months after you disappeared."

Mia saw it immediately and gasped. There, on his left upper shoulder, was a tattoo that shocked her into silence. She reached up a hand and let her fingers trace the marking, her mind flabbergasted. The marking wasn't huge, but it was beautiful. It was a stylized heart with a treble clef symbol, entwined together beautifully. Attached to the heart were two rings, wedding bands. The design was totally inked in black and *Mia* was scrolled above it. Below the design were the words *Real Love Never Dies.*

It was beautiful, and she understood now what his music and his heart were communicating, how the emotions expressed in his playing were connected to her.

Tears sprang to her eyes as she continued to stroke her finger lovingly over the mark. Max had marked himself with her name, too—a testament of his love for her. "But what if you had met someone else? What if—"

Max turned back to her again, picked her up and placed her back on his lap. "There is no one else for me, sweetheart. Even Kade didn't protest when I did it. I guess he got the fact that I needed to do it. He took me to someone he knew who had done a few tattoos for him in the past. He said he already wore a tribute to you every day, but I don't know where he put the tat."

Mia started to laugh. "It's not a tattoo," she informed him cheerfully.

Max looked perplexed. "Then how does he wear a tribute to you?"

"His shirts. He wears those awful shirts," she answered happily. "When I was a kid, he used to always wear black. I told him it was depressing and he should wear something happy. He started picking up outrageous shirts, ones that I'm sure he probably got teased about at school. But he wore them because I liked them, and I told him they were happy shirts. When we grew up, he never stopped. So he does wear something for me. And he never quit wearing them, even when he grew up and I started teasing him about them."

Max frowned. "I always thought he did that to irritate Travis."

Mia laughed. "That's only a side benefit and it might be the reason he does it now. But he started it because of me. I loved them when I was a kid. They were always happy shirts with the most outrageous characters or colors. Honestly, even though I joke around with him, I still love them." She swung around and straddled Max, laying her head on his shoulder. "Tell me why you used to run away. Was it really because of something I did? The way I was acting?"

"No," Max answered quickly, stroking her hair as he responded. "From the time I understood what it meant to be adopted, I was grateful to my mother and father. I knew I'd been thrown away by my real parents, and I was appreciative every day that I had parents who wanted me, who provided all of the things I needed and other things that I didn't need. I was luckier than most of the kids at school, and it wasn't because I was born to them. They chose me. I guess I never wanted them to have a reason to regret it. So I became the perfect child. Or I tried to anyway. I didn't want them to ever have a reason to regret adopting me. When I was really young, I think I was afraid they would give me back or reject me like my natural parents had done."

Mia stroked his neck and back lovingly, imagining the perfect little boy Max had been. Really, it wasn't that hard. The sweet boy had grown into the perfect man. "Didn't you ever want to rebel?" she questioned curiously, wanting to know the real Max instead of the façade.

Max shrugged. "Not really. Even after my parents died, I still wanted to please them. I graduated from college at the top of my class, did everything that was expected of me when I took over my father's business. I even thought of getting into politics because I knew it would make them proud. The only time I wanted to rebel from my normal behavior was when I met you."

"So I was a bad influence?" she asked in a teasing tone.

"Never," he denied, running his hand down her back and wrapping his arms around her waist, holding her closer. "But it made me realize that I wasn't happy before I met you. I was living my life for two people I loved, but I wasn't them. I'd tried to replicate their behavior because I thought being any other way would be a betrayal. I thought I needed to be like them because they were the parents who had wanted me. I was lifted out of a life of poverty because they adopted me. I wanted to be in the same class as my parents, even if I wasn't born into it."

His admission made Mia's heart break. "Just because you're different doesn't mean you aren't still good." Max was the most wonderful man she'd ever known, and she hated that he'd believed he couldn't be perfect if he wasn't exactly like his parents. "I don't think they even expected that."

"I don't think they did either. They would have loved me regardless, because they were good parents," Max answered, his words muffled against her neck. "I expected it of myself."

"And when you met me? I know you had relationships before we met."

"Not like you and me. Before we met, I did the expected things. I dated. I fucked. But I didn't feel the same way. You made me crazy from day one. It knocked me on my ass. I lost my control with you. I'd conditioned myself for years to be a calm, controlled, reasonable businessman like my father, but you blew that persona all to hell, and I was worried about losing you if I wasn't the man you wanted. I knew about your parents, and I knew you needed stability, someone rational and sane," Max admitted gruffly.

"Oh, Max," Mia whispered softly, loving him all the more for being able to talk to her now. "I've never met a saner man, and I kind of like the man you are now." Okay…that was the understatement of the year. His dominant, protective love made her feel safe and adored. "What changed?"

"You died," he answered, his voice tormented. "When I had to start admitting that I'd probably never see you again, hold you again, talk to you again…I hated myself for never letting you know how much you meant to me, that you were my entire world. I fucking regretted every moment I had spent running away when I could have spent that time with you." He released a masculine sigh before continuing, "Now I hate myself for never seeing you, never noticing that you really needed me. I was a selfish prick. Had I stopped worrying about my image, I might have really known you—you might have told me about Danny." He took her head between his hands, his expression tortured. "Believe me, the last thing I wanted was for you to tie yourself in knots trying to please me. Hell, you please me just by breathing. You didn't need to try to be anyone other than who you are."

Mia didn't want him to have regrets. "I know that now. But those were my insecurities, baggage from my past. It wasn't you, Max. We're both responsible for not communicating. We were actually both hiding; in love, but so afraid of losing that love instead of trusting ourselves and each other." God, she must have been blind, deaf, and dumb. The love radiating from his gorgeous eyes was unmistakable. Had she really looked, she would have seen him, really known him. "Growing up in my family was hell. My father's madness and abuse was hard on all of us."

"Your mother never thought about leaving him?" Max asked huskily, putting his forehead against hers in a gesture of comfort.

"No. Never. I think she'd withstood his abuse for so long that she had closed down just to survive. We begged her to leave, even after we were grown, but she wouldn't. She made excuses for his behavior," Mia answered sadly. "I think she loved us, but she couldn't stand up to my father. I'm sure she lived in her own private hell."

Max lowered his hands, running them up and down her upper arms, frowning. "You're cold. You have goose bumps."

Mia suspected it wasn't the cold, but the thrill of sitting here with Max, sharing things they'd never shared before. "Then warm me," she instructed, smiling at his scowl. "We *are* sitting here completely naked."

Stretching out, Max yanked a thick blanket that was draped over the back of the sofa and pulled her over his body, covering her, sandwiching her with warmth as she lay between him and the fleecy covering. "Better?" he asked anxiously.

Mia sighed as she rested her head on his shoulder. "Yes." How could it not be anything other than sublime to be skin to skin with him like this?

"Are you ready to tell me about the asshole who made you run away from me?" It was a question, but Max made it sound more like a demand. "Travis told me the facts. What I want to know is how you felt about him."

Mia wasn't even sure how to explain, but for Max, she'd try. "He didn't start out the way he turned out to be. He was charming, paid attention to me. The controlling behavior started later, a few months after we started dating. The sad part was, it really wasn't all that surprising. It was what I grew up with. He was a lot like my father. I wasn't very strong, Max. I fell into the cycle of abuse. He would apologize and promise never to do it again. But he did. I wanted out, but I guess I wasn't strong enough to fight my way free of him."

"Friends?" Max queried quietly.

"No. Looking back, he managed to slowly, methodically isolate me. I had made friends at school, but he didn't let me hang out with them anymore," she replied regretfully. "I was so relieved when he went to prison. I thought it was over. I left Virginia after school and came back to Florida, hoping to start over again, be smarter."

"Sweetheart, you're brilliant and creative. You were shaped by your past and you were just a kid. Don't blame yourself," Max insisted, running a soothing hand up and down her back. "He came back after he was released from prison, threatened me and your brothers, was ready to blow my brains out? How did you keep him from picking me off? From what I understand, he could have easily made the shot and was crazy enough to do it."

"He was much worse than before," Mia admitted. "He blamed me for everything and was completely delusional. He thought I really wanted to be with him, and he was willing to do anything to get what he wanted. I knew he'd do it." *No more secrets. No more secrets.* "I was unfaithful to you, Max. I'm so sorry." It was the most painful statement she'd ever made, but Max wanted honesty and she needed to tell him the truth.

Max released her, standing up to walk to the fireplace. Bracing his arms against the stone mantel, his head turned away from her, every muscle in his body appeared to tense. Mia held her breath as she watched his profile. He was almost motionless, the only visible movement the rise and fall of his chest as the breath sawed in and out of his lungs unevenly.

Mia's future hung in the balance as she watched him, waiting to see if he would look at her with revulsion, scorn her love for him now. But they needed complete honesty between them, and it was something he deserved to know. She wasn't the same, frightened woman anymore. However, it hadn't made telling him any easier. The changes she'd made in herself just made it possible for her to tell him.

"The bastard raped you, didn't he? He should have gone back to jail." Max turned back to her, his arms dropping to his side, his face filled with rage, his fists clenching and releasing. "Death is too good for a bastard like him."

Mia could feel Max's entire body vibrating with anger, but she realized that he wasn't angry with her. She held out her arms to him, and Max strode toward her, scooping her off the sofa and settling down with her on his lap, his arms tight around her. He hated Danny. And he trusted her, knew she hadn't betrayed him willingly.

"He violated me. He didn't rape me. He wanted me to suck him off...and I did. You were almost on the plane. You just needed a few more minutes. I didn't care, Max. I would have done anything he wanted right at the moment, as long as he didn't hurt you," she told him desperately.

"Fuck! I would rather the bastard had killed me than to force you to do that..." Max's voice trailed off, his face blanching, his expression slowly changing to one of realization. "The night you recovered your memory, in the shower...?"

"I still have nightmares about him. I was dreaming about it, and I woke up with my memory returning. I wanted to replace the bad memories with good ones. And I did," she confessed.

"Shit. That had to be hard. You didn't have to—"

"I wanted to. I wanted to so very badly. And it *was* hard. But it wasn't difficult," she said with a tremulous smile, trying to dispel some of the remorse she could see on his handsome face. "I've always wanted to, but you never seemed to want that, so I stopped trying."

"Oh, baby...I wanted it. I wanted your sweet mouth on me so badly that I knew if it happened, I wouldn't be able to stay controlled," Max told her bluntly.

"It was good," she told him with a tiny smile. "It will keep the nightmares away."

"I'll keep the nightmares away. You'll never have bad dreams again. I'll replace every moment of sorrow you've had with happiness. I swear I will," he said fiercely, though his expression lightened.

Mia doubted that Max could force the Sandman to make all of her dreams good ones, but looking at his display of savage determination, she almost believed he could. And she certainly knew he'd try like hell to do it, even if he had to drag the fabled creature of folklore to their bedside every night to sprinkle magic sand in her eyes. Lifting her arms around his neck, she murmured, "Just love me like this forever. It's enough."

"I'll never stop," he agreed, the tension starting to leave his body. "Just promise me you won't ever try to protect me again. Not at your own expense. I would have rather died than to let him lay a finger on you," he growled.

Mia's eyes filled with tears, the sincerity of Max's statement, a re-avowal of what he'd said earlier, hitting her like a slug to the stomach.

My husband would die for me, just to avoid seeing me hurt.

Knowing she loved him just the same, she answered carefully. "I'm not sure I can make that promise. It wouldn't have saved me, Max. Danny still would have hurt me that day. But it saved you."

He brushed away her concern. "Promise," he insisted.

"No," she refused. "I can't. Could you make the same promise? You said no more lies, and I won't lie to you. I'd protect you if I could."

"Fine," he grumbled. "I'll just make damn sure you're never in a position where you have to make that decision again. And no more running."

She shook her head. "No more running," she agreed.

"If you need to run, I'm going with you," he announced adamantly. "If you had told me you needed to disappear, I would have arranged it...for both of us."

"But your career, your business—"

"Don't mean a damn thing without you. Do you think I'd give a flying fuck about money or anything else if you were in danger? I'd disappear with you, be presumed dead along with you to protect you and your brothers without hesitation." His body tense once again, he shot her a laser-sharp, exasperated look.

Mia sighed, shooting him back an apologetic expression. "I've been through over two years of counseling, and it's still hard to believe someone can love me like you do," she confessed. "I've come a long way, but I'll have my insecure moments," she warned him. "I'll still find it hard to absorb that it's finally over. That we're all safe now." It was hard to comprehend the fact that Max would drop everything in his life for her. Sure, she'd learned to value herself, accept herself the way that she was by working things out with a good counselor, but accepting Max's love was the hardest thing she'd ever done. What had she ever done in this life to deserve him?

"Take all the time you need, baby. I'll convince you eventually," he uttered quietly, his eyes unrelenting as they connected with hers, the love shimmering and flowing white-hot between the two of them, making Mia's pulse hammer.

Stroking his hair, she told him, "You're amazing, Max Hamilton."

"Did you think so when I was smacking your ass?" he asked with a wicked look.

"Yes. It made me want to be naughty all over again," she answered truthfully.

"Sweetheart, I want you to let me know if I ever scare you, or push your boundaries," he warned her dangerously. "My control when it comes to you isn't exactly reliable."

"I'm not afraid of you, Max. And I never could be. I know you'd never hurt me. You make me feel safe." Mia knew she'd never be frightened of Max, no matter how hard he pushed her with his bossiness. The man was an incredible mixture of arrogance and vulnerability, dominance and tenderness, and it fascinated the hell out of her. But she'd never be nervous about any of those qualities. Every part of Max turned her on. He wanted to protect her, and he'd give his life for her. She could never be afraid of *that* kind of love.

"You're safe now, and I'm going to make damn sure you stay that way," he grunted.

They were both silent for a moment, drinking in the pleasure of being together before she asked curiously, "Did Travis kill Danny?"

Max's eyebrows narrowed as he replied, "Probably. It was technically an accident, but Travis was there. Is the fact that he's dead bothering you?"

"No. It doesn't bother me personally that Danny is dead. He deserved it, my family is safe, and it means he won't be around to terrorize anyone else. But poor Travis already put Danny in jail. I hate that he might have had to kill someone for me to be free. He does have a conscience, but he's always done whatever it took to protect me and Kade."

"You know he was the one who put Danny in jail?" Max asked, stunned.

"Of course I knew. Does he really think I'm that stupid? He shows up in Virginia, sees what's happening, and Danny is suddenly going to prison? I knew Travis had done it. What actually happened to kill Danny?" she asked softly.

"When Travis finally located Danny, he went to talk to him. Danny fled in a vehicle and Travis took off after him. Danny ended up going down a very high ravine in Colorado after he lost control during the chase. And believe me, I doubt that Travis felt a twinge of remorse after what the bastard had done to you. When he had verification that Danny was dead, he arranged to bring you home, but apparently never got a chance to talk to you about it because you were gone when he got home from his meeting. Why were you at the picnic anyway?" Max asked, confused. "You had just gotten back to Florida."

"I knew you'd probably be there. I saw the invitation at Travis' house. I knew you'd probably hate me for what I'd done, but I wanted to see you. I couldn't help myself. I kept moving closer, but I didn't think you'd recognize me."

"No chance of that. I could sense you," Max answered, disgruntled. "But the disguise was good enough that no one else did. Did you cut your hair that day?"

"No. I had it done about a year ago. My long hair was used as a weapon too many times. I did it to feel better. It was kind of like therapy. It felt good," she told him.

"He pulled you around by your hair?" Max snarled.

That was putting it mildly, but Mia didn't tell Max that. Her father had done the same thing. She simply answered, "Yes."

Lethargy and exhaustion tugged at Mia's body. Yawning, she closed her eyes.

"Tired?" Max inquired.

"Very. I didn't sleep last night. I wanted to savor the feeling of being together one last time, even though you were three sheets to the wind," she teased. "I can only imagine the whopper of a hangover you must have had this morning. Do you even remember last night?"

"Not much," Max admitted reluctantly.

"Do you want me to fill you in how you accused me of being with another man and how you wanted to hate me?" she teased with a grin. "And why did you bring Tucker? I'm assuming my brothers left and took Tucker with them, but I thought you and my dog barely tolerated each other." Mia knew that wasn't true anymore, but she wanted to hear Max actually admit that he had become buddies with her dog.

"I did think you had a boyfriend. I didn't exactly get the whole story before I laid into your brother. All I heard was that he'd been responsible for taking you away from me. We didn't talk much after that." Max repositioned her so they were lying face to face on the couch, covering both of them with the blanket and wrapping his arms tightly around her. "And the only thing I have in common with that ugly canine is the fact that we both love you. I couldn't leave him at the house alone. I was being humane. He's still a pain in my ass."

"Do you talk to him? Tucker's a good listener," Mia cajoled him.

"He's judgmental. I hate that in a dog," Max grumbled.

She sniggered as she realized that Max was actually talking about Tucker as if the dog were a person. Yep. They had definitely bonded, even if it was an antagonistic relationship. "You adore him," Mia accused.

"He irritates the hell out of me. Blames me because you went away," Max argued.

"You could have dropped him at the neighbor's house," she reminded him. "They love Tucker."

"He wanted to come," Max said grudgingly. "He was whining. He missed you."

Obviously Max wasn't quite ready to admit that he loved Tucker and that the dog had become incredibly attached to him. So she asked, "Did you make peace with Travis?" She stroked her fingers lightly over the black-and-blue mark under his eye.

"Yeah. We've agreed not to kill each other," Max said with a grin.

"And Kade?"

"I still owe him for laughing at my hangover," he replied menacingly.

Mia cringed. "Was it bad?"

"Bad enough to make me want to be a teetotaler. I'm not sure I can ever drink another drop of alcohol again," he answered unhappily. "Now I know why I've never gotten drunk. I had some sense before I met you," he teased. "The thought of you betraying me and happily living your life somewhere else made me crazy. I remember how I felt before I got drunk."

Mia sighed. "I can't believe you've never been drunk. Not even in college?"

"Nope. I studied while everyone else was partying."

"Oh God. You really are perfect," Mia said with mock disgust. "And there could never be anyone else, Max. I even had your name tattooed on my ass," she reminded him jokingly.

Max rubbed the marking possessively. "Yeah. You did. And it's fucking beautiful."

Mia laughed. "I forgot that you curse now, so I guess you aren't perfect."

"I always cursed. I just never did it in front of you. My dad never swore in front of my mother," he replied remorsefully.

"Feel free to let it fly," Mia replied with a smile. "I have two brothers. I've heard every profanity in existence and like to use a few occasionally. But since you never swore, I tried not to let one slip."

"Christ, we really were pathetic. I've always adored you, but I'm not sure we ever really knew each other. No, I take that back. My heart knew you, but the rest of me was a damn idiot," Max answered despondently. "I'm sorry I wasn't there for you when you needed me. You shouldn't have needed to run to Travis. You should have been able to come to me."

Mia put a finger on his lips to shush him. "I didn't allow it. And I wasn't there for you either, Max. But I think we've both changed. Can we just start over again? I'd like to be a real wife to you now."

Max cocked a brow and gave her a bemused look. "Did you really think there was ever any question about it? You're not going anywhere, sweetheart."

Her arrogant and possessive Max was back, and hotter than hell. Mia sighed and squirmed, trying to get closer to him, as close as she could possibly be. She closed her eyes, totally exhausted, but not wanting to miss a moment of this intimacy with him. "You belong to me too, you know."

"Baby, I've known that from the moment we met," he told her seriously, still stroking her tattoo absently.

Mia's heart soared at those words. "Me too," she confessed, knowing that she had started falling for Max at the very beginning, the first time she'd ever seen him smile.

She fell asleep a few moments later, secure in Max's love, in his strong arms. Max sat stroking her tattoo for quite some time with a contented, relieved smile, before he joined her in slumber.

Chapter 12

The next week at the Montana ranch house turned out to be the happiest days of Max's entire life. He and Mia were getting to know each other again—or maybe actually for the very first time. And even as he cherished each day, each new discovery he made about his wife, he still mourned for the wasted years during which he could have really known her, but never did. She was still the sweet, incredible woman he had married, the woman he loved with an intensity that nearly killed him, but she was so much…more. She was complicated and insightful, mysterious and bewildering, and the challenge of figuring out the way her mind worked intrigued the hell out of him. She had shown him the designs she was creating now with her jewelry, and her skill and passion still amazed him. The things she'd never told him in the past because she was afraid he'd be repulsed actually made him admire her strength. His wife was a survivor, a woman who had been through hell and had come out of it stronger and wiser. She might laughingly call herself a "work in progress," but to Max, she was perfect. She always had been.

He sat on the bed and pulled on his hiking boots, a purchase he'd made, along with a bunch of casual clothes, on a trip into Billings. Grinning, he laced the boots, thinking about how seldom he and Mia had even made it out of the house in the last week. But honestly, he didn't think she minded much. She seemed to flash that damned tattoo of hers way too often, and protested very little when he made good on his promise to fuck her every time he saw it.

His cock sprang to life, pressing hard against the denim of his jeans. *Shit. I can't even think about her without getting hard. I don't have to see the damn tattoo to want her.*

Max felt nothing but relief that he didn't have to hide anything from Mia anymore, or worry about not being the man she wanted. Apparently, she wanted him exactly as he was, and her constant affection, the way she opened herself to him, soothed his soul.

Max walked out to the kitchen, stopping at the entryway to watch his wife's sexy ass shimmy around the kitchen while putting their breakfast dishes away, her body swaying to the beat of a country song coming from his cell phone. He'd never heard the song before, and he wasn't much into country, but damned if he'd ever forget the tune now. He might even have to get the music for the piano if there was any possibility he could watch her dance like this whenever he played it.

Mine. My wife. My love. My life. My woman. Forever.

Max couldn't move, almost couldn't breathe as he watched her. How in the hell had he managed to live without her for over two years? He could feel her allure from across the room; the need to be joined with her was constant. Mia completed him, and he'd been lost since the moment she'd left him. Now, he had another chance. Everything he'd ever needed was right here in this room, dancing around in a snug pair of blue jeans and an emerald green sweater.

Mia's head turned, as though she'd sensed his presence, her lips turning up in a brilliant, welcoming smile. God, he loved that about her. There was rarely a time when she didn't look at him that way, like there was nothing that made her happier than seeing *him*. She reached over and switched off the music blasting from his phone, coming over to him and wrapping her arms around his neck. "I hope you don't mind. I used your music app. I left my phone in Florida."

She could use any damn thing she wanted, anything he had. Hell, she could use him for that matter, in any way she wanted to, so long as she kept smiling at him like that. "You're my everything. What's mine is yours," he answered simply, wrapping his arms around her waist.

"So you don't mind if I use your shaver on my legs?" she asked innocently.

"Okay, anything except that," he answered, frowning. He hesitated for a second before adding, "Oh hell, you can use that too. If the blade gets blunt, I'll get another one." Max decided the smile on her face was worth getting a large supply of men's shavers.

Mia's laugh floated around him as she admitted, "I wouldn't dare. I know where men draw the line."

"There are no lines with us," Max answered gruffly. "Cross the line any time you want to with me. Invade my personal space." *Fill my life with love.*

He kissed her because he had to, covering her sweet mouth with his. Mia immediately opened to him, accepted him, welcomed him, and it drove him insane. She melded with him perfectly, beautifully, complying with his needs as if they were her own. Really, maybe they were…but it still inflamed him.

He pulled his mouth from hers and buried his face in her hair, absorbing her scent, needing to be close to her. Maybe he was still afraid someone was going to take her away again, and he'd never survive it.

"I thought we were going riding," Mia murmured against his shoulder.

Both of them were good on horseback. Mia had spent summers here in Montana with her grandmother before the elderly woman had passed away when Mia was in high school. And Max had spent time in Texas with an old friend of his father's when he was alive. They'd spent a few lazy days in the last week riding and enjoying the decent September weather they were getting in Montana. But right now, he was really rethinking the type of riding he wanted

Mia to do. "Maybe we need to take a different type of ride," Max told her huskily, savoring her sweet smell as he gathered her closer.

"I'm glad you said that, because I was thinking the same thing," she answered cheekily. Pulling out of his arms, she took him by the hand and started tugging him toward the front door.

Taken aback, Max followed behind her willingly, trying to figure out if she was thinking of a change of scene for their "ride." He was more than up for anything. Literally.

She led him to the front door and opened it with a huge smile. "Happy birthday, Happy anniversary, merry Christmas," she said, leading him outside.

Max squinted from the bright sunlight, and the glare in front of his eyes. His rental car was gone, and in its place sat a Ferrari 458 Spider, a car he'd considered—but had passed—on buying, even though he'd been salivating over it for a while now. "Whose car is this?"

Mia dangled a set of keys in front of his face. "It's yours now. I wanted to get you something for all the holidays we've missed together. And I know you want it."

Holy shit. Max's jaw dropped and he turned his gaze to Mia as he asked, "How did you know I wanted a Ferrari?" Simon and Sam both had a Bugatti, Kade and Travis had a multitude of man toys, but all Max had ever really wanted was a Ferrari. There was something about the sleek Italian lines of the vehicle that just did it for him.

Mia propped her hands on her hips and gave him a naughty smile. "I was already arranging it before I had to leave the second time. I went to use your laptop a few times, and the screen was up for this car. Obviously you wanted it. Why didn't you just buy it?"

Max drove a Mercedes, a nice sedan that had been moderately priced for that brand. "Because it's not sensible. Why do I need another car, especially one that costs over a quarter million dollars?" He might be a billionaire, but that had never seemed to override his ingrained sense of logic and practicality.

"Max…you can afford it. You can have things you want. You don't have to always do the sensible thing," she teased him softly.

"Sometimes it's fun to do something just because you want to and not try to apply any reason to it."

His eyes roamed over the car longingly. How long had he wanted a Ferrari but never bought one because he didn't actually need it? It was completely impractical, and he fucking loved it. "You did this for me? How did you get it here?" he asked, still stunned.

"With my brother's help. Kade arranged to get it sent here. Do you like it?" she asked nervously. "I paid for it from my own funds."

He didn't care whose funds she used. She was welcome to his money any time she wanted anything. In fact, he would have rather she had spent his money. He had a hell of a lot more than she did, so much that he couldn't spend that much in a lifetime, even if he shopped for luxury products every day. It wasn't the money that had kept him from buying it...it was the senselessness of getting one. "Hell yeah. I love it. I've been wanting a Ferrari forever." He took the keys from her hand and walked over to the vehicle. It was sweet, red with black leather interior, and the top was down. It was an incredible vehicle, and he was itching to take it out on the road.

"You'll rent a sports car, but you won't own one?"

Max grinned at her boyishly, running a hand over the door of the car. "I had to scratch the itch occasionally."

Mia wrapped her arms around him, hugging his back as she murmured, "It's permanently cured now."

Max turned and hefted her up against him. Mia wrapped her legs around his waist, bringing their faces level. "I have another itch," he told her wickedly, ready to wait for the ride in his new vehicle. "I can't believe you did this for me. How is it that you seem to know what I want before I do?"

"Observation," she told him with a laugh. "I spied this time. And you knew you wanted it; you just wouldn't admit it to yourself. You've spent a lot of senseless money on me in the past, but you make different rules for yourself."

Max wasn't sure, but he was pretty certain it was more than observation. Mia got him in a way he didn't even comprehend himself.

"I actually got something for you, too." And he hoped she liked it. "And spending money on you is never senseless."

"What?" she asked curiously, placing a tender kiss to his lips before unwrapping her legs from his waist, her feet landing gracefully on the ground.

Max nearly groaned aloud, the loss of having her so close to him almost painful. "I got it in Florida." Digging in his pocket, he pulled out a black velvet box. Nervously, he opened the lid. "I didn't know if we'd find your wedding ring again. So I got this."

The ring had a platinum band completely covered in diamonds, an enormous sapphire on top embedded into a heart crafted of the same precious metal and surrounded completely by more diamonds.

"Oh, Max." Mia sounded breathless as she took the box, her hand trembling. "It's incredible. But I have my wedding ring."

"You have another finger," Max reminded her with a small smile. "One ring for our first marriage, and another for our second chance." He pulled the ring from the box in her hand and slipped it over the ring finger of her other hand. "Keep me," he demanded, not really wanting it to be a question. He was definitely keeping *her*.

Her expression stunned, she looked up at him with tears on her face. "This is exquisite. It must have cost you a fortune. The sapphire is at least seventeen carats."

Max had forgotten for a moment that he was married to a jewelry designer who knew her gems, even though she wasn't working with precious stones much anymore. "Cost isn't exactly a problem. I wanted more diamonds, but Gabrielle said it would be overkill."

"Gabrielle. Oh, God. I knew this looked like her work. But she's booked forever for custom stuff. How did you get her to do this so quickly?"

Max had needed to shell out a lot of cash and do some groveling to get the famous jewelry designer to make Mia's ring a priority, but he would have paid anything to get it, and have it on Mia's finger as quickly as possible. After seeing the way she had mourned the loss of her ring, he would have given his entire fortune to get her another one. "Do you like it?" he asked anxiously, not wanting to discuss the price or how he'd gotten it so quickly.

Mia touched the ring reverently, her eyes shimmering. "There isn't a woman in the world who wouldn't. Thank you, Max. I love it. I love you."

"Don't cry." He wiped the tears from her face gently. "It was supposed to make you smile."

"I am happy. It's just such an incredible piece of jewelry. You didn't need to do this. I already have a gorgeous wedding ring."

"You didn't have to buy me a Ferrari," he reminded her.

"I wanted to," she argued.

"Ditto," he said, grinning at her.

"Are you planning on giving me a ride?" she asked softly, her eyes drifting to his new car.

Oh yeah. He wanted to give her the ride of her life right now. Max was seriously considering laying her over the hood of the Ferrari naked, but Mia had already jogged to the passenger side of the car and hopped over the door and into the sports car.

Resigned, he opened the door and sank into the leather seat, starting the vehicle and turning it around so he could head out to the highway. He drove slowly down the driveway, trying to avoid the potholes, and making a mental note to get them filled in as soon as possible.

"Do we know where we're going?" Max asked Mia, not certain exactly where the back highways led in the area or what his destination was going to be.

"Does it matter?" Mia asked, her hair ruffling in the breeze as he stopped at the end of the driveway.

Max frowned as he looked back at her. He'd never been a fly-by-the-seat-of-his-pants type of guy. He always knew exactly where he was going, what he was doing, and why he was doing it.

But I'm in a car I've dreamed about since I was a teenager, with a beautiful woman in the passenger seat—a woman who I love and thought I'd never be able to touch again.

So no…hell no…he didn't care where he was going, as long as Mia was going with him.

His whole body relaxed as he looked at Mia, her face radiant and glowing, his scowl disappearing and his lips curling up into a boyish grin. "Nope. It doesn't matter at all."

"You look like a teenage boy who just got his driver's license," Mia observed, amused.

"I've had a license for a long time, woman. But I do feel like a teenager in a couple of ways," he told her hoarsely, his mouth going dry as he looked at her.

"How?"

"I want to see if this vehicle really does go from zero to sixty in less than four seconds and you make me as horny as a teenage kid who wants nothing more than to get into the panties of the girl sitting beside him," he answered, shooting her dangerous look.

"I'm pretty easy for you," Mia answered in low, sultry voice. "I'm your wife." She paused before telling him sweetly, "Turn right. It's a long stretch of pretty straight road."

She might be his wife, but she'd never be easy. Luckily, his woman had been referring to sex, and in that regard, he was all for her being easy…with him. Mia would also tease him, delight him, frustrate the hell out of him, and change him in ways that would always make him a better man. She'd push his boundaries, make him realize that he could shed his Mr. Perfect title and still be a man his adoptive parents would be proud of if they were still alive. He'd probably never be reckless or completely abandoned, because that wasn't who he really was, but he was learning that everything in life didn't have to make sense. And in fact, most of the really good things, stuff that made life really worth living, actually didn't involve reason or logic.

Turning his eyes back to the road, he let himself simply enjoy the purr of the powerful engine as he turned onto the two-lane highway. There wasn't a car in sight, and there usually wasn't until one reached the freeway. The ranch was a fairly lengthy drive from Billings, and the area was sparsely populated.

"Zero to sixty in under four seconds," Max said absently to himself, driving slowly as he contemplated the road ahead of him and got the feel of the new vehicle.

"Well, let's see it, Grandpa. Tear it up. Just watch for deer," Mia said happily, sounding more than ready to see him speed it up.

Max accelerated, the car responding with a roar as the powerful engine shot the vehicle down the pavement, the horsepower beneath the sleek hood making the speed climb rapidly.

Forty miles per hour.
Fifty miles per hour.
Sixty miles per hour.

"Damn, it really does," Max said loudly enough for Mia to hear over the wind and the engine.

His wife simply laughed, a loud *whoop* that kept him accelerating until he felt like he was flying. He pushed the vehicle as far as he dared with his wife beside him…but later, when he was alone, he'd test it more. But not with his entire life sitting beside him. He might be loosening up, but he wasn't stupid. Slowing back to a little above the speed limit, he desperately wished he could find the words to say to Mia. It wasn't the gift of the vehicle that moved him, but the fact that she wanted to make him happy.

"Turn up here. The next right," she instructed him excitedly.

Max didn't ask where they were going. He still didn't care. He turned right and Mia directed him through a few more turns before she had him pulling into a dirt parking area.

After he got out of the car, he caught Mia just as she was about to hop out of the convertible, grasping her around the waist and swinging her over the door, savoring the feel of her body against him. He let her lower her feet to the ground, not sure if he wanted to let go.

"This is one of my favorite spots. I want you to see it," Mia told him as she grabbed his hand enthusiastically and pulled him along behind her, leading him down a footpath.

Bemused, Max let her lead, enjoying the view from behind.

They didn't go far before they started walking up a steep incline that ended in a spectacular view. Surrounded by evergreens, the elevated spot provided the perfect view of several mountain ranges and the feeling that one could see forever.

Max saw the drop-off warning as he came up next to Mia, putting his arms around her waist as he looked down at a good one hundred foot vertical drop right below them.

"I love it here," Mia said softly. "I used to come here when I was really lonely."

The vulnerability in her voice tugged at Max's heart. "How often was that?" he wondered aloud, resting his head against her hair, hating the fact that Mia had ever been lonely. But he knew exactly how she'd felt.

"Every day," she admitted sadly, covering his hands that were resting around her waist with hers and sighing contentedly. "There wasn't a day that I didn't miss you."

Max tried to swallow the lump that was swelling in his throat, unable to express in words exactly how desolate he had been without her. Failing to find the right verbalization, he turned her in his arms and tipped her face up, lowering his mouth to hers with a hungry groan. She tasted like mint, mocha coffee, and sunshine, and Max indulged decadently, his tongue entering and retreating, savoring every flavor of Mia. She opened and merged her mouth with his, releasing a tiny moan that almost made Max completely lose it. Kissing Mia was like drinking, but never completely quenching his thirst.

She's mine.

And Max was determined never to screw that up again. Pulling his lips from hers, he told her in a graveled voice, "I love you. I missed you so much I didn't feel like I was alive anymore. I need you, Mia." No more bullshit, no pretending like he didn't crave her constantly, like he didn't long to claim her all the damn time.

No running away. Not anymore. Not for either one of them.

She pulled away panting, her breathing audible. "Your kisses are dangerous," she said in a teasing voice, skipping backward as she smiled at him.

Mia had no more than spoken the words when the earth began to crumble beneath her feet. Max lunged, realizing she was too close to the edge of the cliff, but his hands came up empty as Mia plunged downward, disappearing before he could get a good grasp on her sweater.

All Max heard was his wife's horrified scream, and then she was gone.

Chapter 13

M ia trembled as she clung to the bush protruding from the side of the cliff, her feet precariously placed on what had to be a small ledge made of the jagged rock that formed the large precipice.

Breathe, Mia. Breathe. You aren't dead...yet.

Trying to shake off the momentary paralysis caused by the terror of the fall, she tried to assess the situation. And it wasn't easy. Hanging perilously, with very little between her and a very long, deadly fall, didn't exactly help her to clear her head.

"Mia!" Max's tortured bellow brought Mia back to reality.

Slowly tilting her head, she could actually see Max's head above hers, the proximity of him comforting. His anguished gaze met hers as she carefully let go of the bush with one hand and reached out her arm. Max lowered his body and reached for her, but there was still too much distance between them.

So close, but not close enough.

"Fuck. I'm coming down," she heard Max say harshly.

Panicked, she gripped the bush again. "No, Max. Go for help." The vertical drop would kill anyone who fell. She'd looked down on this view enough times to know there was nothing but rock beneath them. There were very few decent handholds on this rocky cliff, and she was clinging to one of them, the rocks beneath her feet unsteady. "You can't climb down. You'll go down. Please."

Mia no longer cared if she plunged down the cliff, but she could not bear to see it happen to Max.

"Like hell," Max replied rigidly, swinging his lower body over the edge. "You can't hang on that long."

No…she probably couldn't. The bush was the only thing keeping her on the face of the rocks. The ledge under her feet merely took some of the weight from her arms. "Max! Damn it. Stop." Seeing him start to carefully descend made her heart skip a beat, the organ stopping for a torturous moment as he found unpredictable footholds.

"You're not fucking dying here, sweetheart. Not today. Not on any day. I just got you back," he replied, his voice guttural and raw.

She couldn't see his face, but he was determined, and at the moment she was cursing his tenacity. "This is crazy. We'll both die."

"Nobody. Is. Dying," Max grunted, moving slowly down beside her, grasping another small branch hanging from the rocks as he came level with her body.

Mia gasped for air, her fear getting the best of her. Max was barely clinging to the rocks, his grip even less stable than hers. Her terrified eyes met his, and his hazel eyes held a liquid fire—a driven, feral, and resolute look that she'd never seen before on his handsome face. "Max. Please." Tears streamed down her face, her whole body quivering from the knowledge that Max didn't give a damn whether he died trying to save her sorry ass. She'd gotten them into this situation by stupidly stepping too close to the edge, but Max hadn't hesitated to come after her. "Stubborn, pigheaded man," she whispered desperately. "You're supposed to be the cautious one."

"Not when it comes to you," Max answered grimly. "You're going up, sweetheart."

"Max. You can't—"

He put a hand under her ass and hefted her body upward, moving to take her place as he pushed. "Climb, dammit," he demanded, spotting her from underneath her body.

She wasn't far from the top, and Max's stern voice made her scramble to find a hold above him to keep him from falling. One final mighty push from beneath her sent her upper body over the top of the cliff, and she clawed her way over, panting and breathless as she collapsed on solid ground.

She swung her body around awkwardly, hanging her head over the edge of the cliff and gasped as she spotted Max just as the foothold she had been standing on gave way, collapsing beneath his foot. He'd put too much weight on the wobbly rocks when he'd shoved her over the edge, and his body swung insecurely for moment, the longest moment of Mia's life, until he found purchase again.

Please. Please. Don't let him die.

She nudged her upper body slowly over the ledge, trying to get closer to him.

"Get your ass back over that edge now," Max commanded gratingly, finding another handhold and inching his powerful body upward.

Mia inched back, but not much, determined to help Max. "You can grab my hand."

"Just. Move. Back." Max's voice was rough, his powerful body moving up the cliff from pure male strength and stubborn will.

Realizing that her immovable husband wasn't going to risk pulling her over, Mia moved sideways, leaving him space to launch himself over the edge as he found a foothold to help him mobilize. She grabbed the waistband of his jeans and tugged with all her might as his upper body hit the rim of the cliff.

She gasped as he grabbed her around the waist and rolled, protecting her with his body as they moved away from the edge of the jagged rock wall. He didn't stop until they hit grass, coming to rest against the trunk of a tree, her body sprawled on top of him.

He got up and pulled her to her feet, his eyes shooting fire. "Are you okay?" he asked abruptly, his hands everywhere on her body at once, checking for injuries.

Mia expelled a pensive breath, her body still shaking. Max was scraped and scratched, but he was all in one piece. "I'm fine. I was just afraid you'd kill yourself. What were you thinking?" she asked, adrenaline firing through her body as she shot him an angry look. "That was a stupid, risky thing to do. Don't you ever do that again, Maxwell Hamilton. You took at least twenty years off my life and scared the shit out of me." She punched him in the shoulder. And then did it again, relief coursing through her that she was punching the solid muscle that was Max.

Max picked her up calmly as she continued to punch at him, carrying her flailing body down the incline, stopping about halfway down and setting her gently on her feet. He captured her wrists and pinned her against an enormous tree, subduing her with very little effort.

Her adrenaline still high, she stopped punching at him and started to sob, her fear overtaking every one of her emotions. "What would I do if something happened to you, Max? I couldn't stand it."

"I know. That's how I felt for over two years when I thought you were dead, baby," Max answered, his voice coarse and raw.

Mia stopped struggling, the truth of the hell Max had really been through hitting her straight in the gut. She'd had a few minutes of agony, wondering if Max was going to die. He'd had over two years of not knowing, thinking she was already dead. She'd been lonely, mourning Max, but at least she'd known he was still alive. "I couldn't have borne it. I'm sorry. I'm so sorry." The full force of what Max had suffered filled her with remorse, anguish, and grief.

"I don't care about the past anymore, Mia. I care about us now. If I have you now, nothing else matters. I get that you were trying to protect me. I get that you didn't know what else to do. I contributed to the whole mess with my own fucked-up way of handling everything. Let it go. Right now I need to be inside you," Max growled, grasping the bottom of her sweater to pull it over her head. "We're alive, we're together."

"I can't believe you came down that cliff after me," she told him, still stunned.

"It doesn't matter where you are—I'll always come after you," Max vowed gruffly.

She looked up at Max's crazed, anguished, and yearning expression, and her entire body went up in flames. Max was feeling the rush of adrenaline too, but his needed to be vented in an entirely different way.

Mia's core flooded with heat, her need answering his, and they were suddenly clawing at each other to get naked, get closer. Clothing hit the ground as they disrobed each other in a frenzy, both of them perfectly aware that they could have just died and never experienced this closeness again.

"Be still," Max told her harshly, pinning her hands over her head against the tree when they both were finally naked.

Mia was panting heavily, her pussy flooding at the command in Max's voice. She complied immediately, her body relaxing as she looked up at his fierce expression with feminine longing. Her husband might have been reluctant to admit his alpha tendencies toward her, but there was no mistaking the possessive, protective, and insanely covetous look on his face right now. All of the dominant emotions were there in glorious abundance, contained in her hot, muscular male standing directly in front of her, the testosterone seeping from every pore of his sculpted body.

His skin was scratched and sweaty, droplets of perspiration rolling down his face as he pinned her with a hungry look. "I need you to need me," he said huskily, one hand gripping both her wrists as the other caressed one of her breasts, circling the nipple with his thumb.

Mia whimpered, both nipples hard and incredibly sensitive, the slightest touch jarring her nerve endings. "I already do. Fuck me, Max. Please."

"Do you know how I felt when you went over that cliff, sweetheart?" he asked gruffly as his fingers moved to the other breast, pinching it lightly before soothing it with his fingers.

"Yes," Mia cried out. "The same way I felt when I saw you hanging there."

"I felt like you were dying all over again." Max's hand moved slowly between her breasts and down her quivering belly. "And I died for a moment too."

His voice was harsh, but his touch was gentle as it moved between her thighs, tenderly parting her folds and stroking lightly.

It wasn't enough, and Mia's body started to protest, her hips moving forward, needing more pressure, *more Max*. "I need you," she said longingly, moaning as his fingers brushed her clit, teasing her.

"You're wet for me, sweetheart. But I want you needier," he said quietly against her ear, nipping at the lobe and running his tongue along her flesh. "I want you to come for me. Because I know that once I'm inside you, I won't last. Not this time."

Mia moaned, needing his touch more than she needed anything else on earth. Max wanted her to be satisfied, and he was putting her needs first. But she wanted him inside her, needed to be connected to him. "Then make me come. Because I have to have you inside me now," she shouted at him, not caring who heard her.

Max shuddered, as though he had lost control, and took her mouth, his fingers playing between her thighs like he played the piano: strong, confident, and absolutely perfect. He searched and found the engorged bud that needed his attention, sliding over it with powerful strokes as his tongue plundered her mouth, never letting up on the pressure until she detonated, her whole body shuddering as her climax hit her with an explosive intensity that shattered her completely.

Pulling his mouth from hers, Max unshackled her wrists and cupped her ass. "Put your arms and legs around me," he ordered, not even letting her take a breath before he buried himself inside her with a masculine groan. "Nothing between us this time. You feel incredible. So damn good."

Mia obediently wrapped her legs around his waist and put her arms around his neck, gasping as he plunged inside her, burying himself to the balls. She knew he was trying to keep her back off the tree to keep from hurting her back, but she couldn't have cared less if she got a few scrapes. The feeling of having him deeply embedded inside her was all-consuming and she was too impassioned to care. "Yes," she encouraged him, running her tongue over his neck and nipping his skin, glorying in his savage growl of approval as he pulled back and entered her again. Harder. Stronger. Deeper.

Mia gasped with every powerful stroke of his cock, his groin pumping against her sensitive clit as he hammered her with thrust after thrust, every forward movement more frantic and furious. She felt her orgasm rushing up to meet her, raw and forceful, so overwhelming that she screamed, "I love you."

Max groaned and shuddered as he pumped his hips desperately inside her, the walls of her channel clenching his cock, milking him as she came helplessly.

Mia grasped his head and kissed him, moaning into his mouth as her body exploded in a blast of heat that felt like she was combusting. She was delirious and drunk with pleasure as Max's tongue met hers, entwining and joining them together in every possible way, their bodies rocking as they stayed locked together in a world that belonged only to the two of them.

Max lowered them to a patch of grass, keeping her on top of him, their lips still touching and tasting as he speared a hand into her hair and kept the other possessively on her ass, absently stroking over her tattoo.

Completely spent, Mia rested her head on Max's shoulder, murmuring softly, "You scared the hell out of me. Don't do it again." She tried to put some kind of conviction in her voice, but she was too tired.

"Sweetheart, if it sends you into that kind of passionate rage, I think I'll do it every day," he said with a masculine chuckle.

"I'll divorce you," she claimed weakly.

"No you won't," he answered in a cocky tone, stroking her hair gently.

"How do you know?" she answered cheekily.

"Because you love me," he reminded her confidently.

"Yeah. I do." Mia was so satiated that she didn't even want to argue. He was right. No matter what happened, they'd always be together. She kind of thought it had been fated from the moment she had ruined his expensive suit, looked up at Max, and saw her destiny in his gorgeous hazel eyes. "Do you realize we're actually outside and naked? This really isn't good for your image, you know."

"You shot my famous Hamilton control all to hell the moment I met you," Max grumbled. "No more Mr. Perfect for me."

"Do you care?" Mia asked him curiously, wondering if he resented losing a little of his old image—the reasonable, calm, respectable Max that he used to be.

She pulled back to look at his face. He had a happy, silly grin on his face that made her heart skitter.

"Hell no. I'm starting to learn that being a little bit wicked is a lot more fun." He kissed her gently and brought them both to their feet.

They dressed quickly, laughing as they brushed grass and leaves from each other. Max took her hand as they descended the rest of the hill and helped her into his new car.

He drove the speed limit all the way home. Mia teased him about being a grandpa, but when he answered that there was only so much a man like him could take in one day, she smiled.

Max wasn't perfect, but he was damn close. And he was hers. A woman couldn't get much luckier than that.

Leaning back in the plush leather seat with a sigh, Mia realized that after all the pain and heartache of the last few years, she was finally joined with Max the way they were always meant to be together. And if she was with Max, wherever they happened to be geographically, she would always be home.

Epilogue

One Month Later In Tampa

Max looked at the file on his desk with a frown, wondering if what he saw in the information it contained was even feasible. Was it really possible that he and Maddie had another sibling? He'd been digging, trying to make sure he didn't have more family out there somewhere in the world. Although he was completely satisfied with his life now, he didn't want to have another sibling out there who he didn't know about. If he hadn't checked every possibility, he'd always wonder. So he'd let investigators continue to dig for answers. His natural mother had been married two more times after his father had died. It had been entirely possible that she'd had other children. The information was sketchy, but he needed to investigate this possibility, check out the information his agents had recently uncovered.

"Yeah. No problem. I can check it out," Kade said casually, his voice emanating from the speakerphone on the desk of Max's home office.

"It's pretty unlikely, but I have to check, and I'm not ready to leave Mia again so soon. I can't," Max admitted in a husky voice to his brother-in-law. "And she has projects that she has to complete."

Kade's groan echoed through the room over the phone connection. "You two need to knock that crap off eventually."

Hell. Max hoped they never did. Even though he knew exactly what Kade was talking about, he asked innocently, "What?"

"The disgustingly in love stuff. It's getting nauseating," Kade answered in a disgruntled voice.

Max looked up as Mia entered the room, looking gorgeous in a sexy red dress that made his cock instantly hard. "Mia's ready. We're out of here. We need to get to a charity function. Thanks for helping me out. I'll have what I've got sent over to you," Max told Kade absently, reaching out to disconnect the call.

Coming to his feet, Max brushed the arms of his tux, never taking his eyes off his wife as he met her in the middle of the room.

The last month had been a time of exploration and discovery for them. Every day he thought there was no way he could love his wife any more than he already did. But every single day, he tumbled just a little deeper in love with the incredible woman standing in front of him, a woman who had bared her soul to him over the last month, and allowing him to do the same. They were close in a way they had never been before, sharing the joy and the gut-wrenching emotion of a love so strong it was almost terrifying. Almost...but not quite. The ecstasy was definitely worth a little fear. For him, Mia was worth everything.

"You look beautiful." He knew the words were inadequate. She looked amazing. The red silk cocktail dress flirted with her knees, the material hugging her curves intriguingly.

"You're looking pretty gorgeous yourself, Mr. Hamilton," Mia said flirtatiously, straightening the bow tie of his tux. "Are we ready?"

"Whenever you are, sweetheart. Are you sure you're okay with this? I know you aren't particularly fond of these events. But if somebody irritates you, tell them exactly what you think."

Honestly, Max didn't think his wife had much of a problem doing that anymore.

Max knew that Mia only agreed to go with him to these types of events because he had to go, but she attended with him anyway. He was grateful that she stayed at his side, but he didn't want her to continue doing something she didn't like to do to please him.

"I'm fine with it. It's something you need to do and I want to be with you," she told him calmly. "I'm ready," she said suggestively, turning toward the door.

Max's jaw dropped as he saw the back of her dress. Or rather, when he saw that her dress pretty much had no back. The front of the dress was deceivingly demure, but the back was completely unacceptable. "You aren't wearing that?" Max said, but it was a question rather than a statement.

"You don't like it?" she questioned innocently, winking at him cheekily.

Hell yes...he liked it. Every male within viewing distance would love it. The back dipped down to the top of her ass, showing an abundance of smooth, creamy skin. "I love it. And so will every other guy at the ball. I'll end up in a brawl by the end of the night," he grumbled, but his mouth was dry and his breath caught as he watched the silk sway temptingly near the curve of her ass.

"I don't care about any other guy. I only care what you think," she told him bluntly.

Max moved forward slowly, staring at the expanse of exposed skin on her back with a covetous, possessive look.

She's mine. She always has been and always will be.

"How exactly do you wear undergarments with that?" he asked in a husky voice, pretty certain he didn't want to know the answer.

"It's a little tricky. Honestly...I can't. They don't work with this dress," she replied nonchalantly as she headed for the door.

I was afraid she was going to say that.

Max caught up to her at the door, his hand moving to the back of the dress, nudging it gently aside. It only took a little nudge to expose her tattoo. "Damn. You know what that does to me."

"I know. But it's covered," she reasoned.

It didn't matter to Max. He still knew it was there, and he was looking at it right now. "You remember what I said," he rumbled in a warning voice.

"I do," Mia said, turning to shoot him a *fuck-me* smile.

She was reeling him in, and she had him: hook, line, and sinker. "I'm a man of my word," he told her dangerously. "And we'll be late for the ball." Not that he cared. His balls were blue, and who the hell would really miss him anyway?

"It won't exactly be the first time." Mia turned and put her arms around his neck.

Max was a goner, but he didn't even try to hide it. He scooped her into his arms and kissed her as he carried her to their bedroom, Mia's laughter echoing throughout their huge home, a home that was now completely filled with love.

They weren't late for the ball; they never even went.

Max sent an apology the next day, but it was just a formality, a note claiming something urgent had come up. Really, he wasn't actually sorry at all, and the excuse wasn't exactly a lie. But he couldn't tell the whole truth…that they had never made it out of the house that night all because of a silky red dress, a sexy tattoo, and a certain something that really had urgently come up!

~*~ *The End* ~*~

The Billionaire's Obsession Series:

The Billionaire's Obsession –
The Complete Boxed Set (Simon's Story)

Heart Of The Billionaire –
(The Billionaire's Obsession ~ Sam)

The Billionaire's Salvation –
(The Billionaire's Obsession ~ Max)

Coming Soon: October 20, 2013 –
The Billionaire's Angel
(The Billionaire's Obsession - A Christmas Story)
This story will be included in a Christmas duet with
Cali Mackay entitled "A Maine Christmas...Or Two"

Coming Soon: November, 2013 –
The Billionaire's Game
(The Billionaire's Obsession ~ Kade)

For visit me at:

Please visit me at:
http://www.authorjsscott.com
http://www.facebook.com/authorjsscott
Twitter: @AuthorJSScott
Email: jsscott_author@hotmail.com

Made in the USA
San Bernárdino, CA
30 November 2016